Reshma Baig

The Memory of Hands

Reshma Baig was born in Dar es Salaam, Tanzania and came to the United States when she was four. She studied African-American Literature as a Mellon Scholar at Cornell University and earned an MS Ed. in Counseling from Hunter College. In 1995, she was recognized by the Brooklyn Superintendency as an exemplary New York City teacher. She teaches and counsels adolescents and adults in New York City.

To 'Mrs. Laffin,
with warm wishes
from: Sawleka, Meher,
& baby boy
Abbas.

The Memory of Hands

Reshma Baig

New York

PUBLISHER'S NOTE:

This is a work of fiction. Names, characters, places, and incidents either are the product of the author's imagination or are used fictitiously, and any resemblance to actual persons, living or dead, events, or locales is entirely coincidental.

For the sake of brevity, an asterisk after the usage of the word [Prophet] denotes peace be upon him (p.b.u.h.), respectfully.*

Cover concept & Imaging: Caterina Barone
Collage by Reshma Baig
First print: August 1998

Published and distributed by:
International Books & Tapes Supply
PO Box 5153
Long Island City, NY 11105, USA
Tel: (718) 721 4246
Fax: (718) 728 6108
e-mail: itsibts@aol.com
www.itsibts.com
Manufactured in the United States of America

ISBN 1-889720-27-5

For the two whose strength is in my bones,
For the one who is my companion
in this life and the next,
For the one whose difference
is mirror image,
and
Always for the One
in whose Eyes
I find limitless mercy.

"On the Day of Judgment,
their tongues, and their hands, and their feet,
will bear witness to what they have done [on Earth]."
- Qur'an 24:24

Contents

Prologue: In the Palm of Your Hand   1

1. Garden Angels   9

2. Tickets to Heaven   23

3. 2-205   39

4. Monster's Request   53

5. Coverings   65

6. Matrimonials   81

7. The Charismatic   105

8. A Doctor in the Family   135

9. Professionals   169

10. Dear Teacher   183

Epilogue: Vision Scribes   195

Prologue:

In the Palm of Your Hand

❦

❖❖❖

I sit with my little sister on the bank of a moody river. We watch the cool current slip slide over rocks and trip over the riddles of broken branches and painted turtles. Our naked toes burrow in and out of mud as thick and black as burnt caramel.

Nearby, a navy-blue beetle has accidentally fallen on his back. His little legs kick the air like spindly children's arms waving through school bus windows. After placing him on the palm of my hand, I see that his shell is iridescent. Like mother of pearl. Like the wet, fragile skin of a soap bubble. His feet ramble over the thick scratches of dirty highway on my hands. Prickly feelers sting with sharp tickles, but I am not afraid. I will not drop him. Slowly, carefully, he stops to take rest on the round of my hand. He is fearless, anticipating safety on some foreign terrain offered by an unknown friend.

I hold the beetle close to my face and see him smile. My sister says bugs don't smile, but I know a smile when I see one. At least he's happy now that he is back on his feet. He may have been off to do something important and is probably eager to get on his way.

My father once told me that bugs are very busy creatures. "They always have something to do," he said, "and they know they have very little time."

I hope this beetle remembers this favor. He may pick me up one day when I've fallen on my back. As he walks away, he turns around and nods his head. We will know each other from now on. He will remember me. We have seen one anothers' faces.

As my new friend walks away, I turn to see that my other sister, my secret sister, is collecting river water in a jar on the opposite bank. Her cotton pants are rolled up to her knees as she bends to dip the mouth of the jar into the river. Perched upon two broken rocks, her hair falls into her face as she fills the jar with clear, cold water. She carries the jar to a pebbly clearing near the bank where a small tree has been uprooted. When she turns around, she sees us across the way.

My little sister starts to swing her legs, and the water starts to splatter in our faces. We wave to the girl across the water. We want her to join us. She is our secret sister. Even though we've seen her a thousand times, we still aren't quite sure what she looks like, except for her eyes. We know her eyes. No one can see her unless they want to, unless they fear nothing except the truth.

My little sister points to her and says, "Look at her big brown eyes. Look at her. You can see it in her eyes."

"See *what* in her eyes?" I ask.

"Our minutes and hours. Moments smaller than this lady bug here, and larger than the boulder which stands on that hill."

Our secret sister, the one we call Time, the one who kissed us and witnessed our birth, has been with us all along. She always confuses us since she never looks the same except for her eyes. She is sister to fossils, prophets and butterflies. A barefoot thief who runs over grass and broken shells just to bring us some golden rays in a basket of sky each morning before breakfast.

Time always tells me that she loves my mother, that she has known her for ages. But she has other mothers as well, as many as can see her, perhaps. And we too will see them all when we close our eyes for the last time.

My little sister is afraid of closing her eyes for the last time. As we lie awake under our blankets at night, she always says the same thing. "Maybe I won't be able to open them again after tonight."

I tell her to close her eyes. "You see. There's still so much to see. There's nothing to be afraid of when you close your eyes. It's just a doorway, a door you never saw until you found yourself in the dark."

When she wakes up in the morning, she tells me that the first thing she saw when she closed her eyes was our secret sister's eyes. She says they look like giant honey marbles; clear and brown like they are now as she wades through the river to join us.

Although Time carries a jar full of river water on her head, she wades through with speed and throws her arms up in joy. She begins to laugh as my little sister runs to the shallow end of the river to meet her.

Time greets my little sister and puts the jar in her hands. My sister looks at the universe of little fish, sand and bits of rock swirling in the jar. Time sits at the bank, rolls down the folds of her pants and places a few odd shaped pebbles in her pockets. "They have many stories to tell," she says as she bends her ears down to make sure there aren't other stories resting under her feet.

She is satisfied knowing that she has collected her stories for today. She pauses for a moment to take a big breath of air and then starts to move her shoulders up and down.

Her skin is transparent and starts to move slowly, like a breeze is winding its way up from inside her bones.

Time smiles and tells us it is once again the hour of change. "Look away for a moment my dear sisters. I'll let you watch when you're older, but for now, please be patient. You know me. You know what I was sent to do. I am a witness and have some instructions. Please, keep your smiles on your face. Don't look sad. I will be done in a moment."

We do what our secret sister says. We do not question her because something bad cannot have such light. We turn around to face the trees for a moment, but my little sister cannot wait. She has to see. She never listens to anyone, not even Time. And for her, an invitation *not* to look is as good as one which implores you to stare.

Time's skin comes off softly. Beautiful words molt and fall to the ground in thin layers like leaves of lucid parchment. The words, petals of prayers large and small, are so light that at first they hover over the ragged bank for a second, then quickly fall to melt into the river like flakes of whispering talc. I know they will reach the sidewalk near my house when it rains. My mother told me that water is all the same. It all blends to form one sea. That it all comes from the same home: the sky.

Suddenly, there is a noise up above. My sister and I stand still, eyes glared at the sky, mouths frozen in perfect O's. Frightened birds quickly flutter off branches as a thunder clap brings an argument to the sky. The sun negotiates a peaceful offering, a compromise. Sunbeams join hands with water droplets and gentle rain falls.

As a sun shower begins to trickle on the tops of our heads, my sister points to the river. Time has descended into the water. She was right here before us a minute ago—we didn't even see her move. We quickly wade into the river, and the water cradles our knees in a gentle rocking. A few feet from where we stand, we can see hollow shapes moving in the liquid belly of the river. We see the rapid break of secret flapping fins, signs of a gracefully determined fish under the surface of the water. We cannot see Time, but we know she is still there. She has simply taken on the color of the rain. And although we are only seven and nine, we know you cannot see the rain after it has entered the folds of a river, but you can catch it and hold it for a moment or two in the palm of your hand.

Garden Angels

❖❖❖

*It's not a specific feature that Zafran focuses on when she sees her
mother's face in her dreams. Rather than looking at her face, her
eyes settle upon the various colors that rise like incandescent tales
from her cheekbones and circle in dusky halos around her eyes.*

*From far away, her mother's face appears to be a garden.
A small universe of color and light softly stumbling from limb,
branch, petal, to thorn and round again to the roses that compose
the patchwork on her cheek. While a rain of salty, silky sweat
forms at the velvety points of each brow, she looks closer at that
garden of a face. Her mother's skin is earth tilled by joy, laughter,
pain and composure. There are never any tears because an elegant
woman never cries. She just puts a cutting of sweetgrass or a
wildflower's scented husk behind her ear and walks on.*

•❖•

Sonyah's scribes sit upon her shoulders wearing white kurtas
yellowed and frayed at the ends. Their small hands finger the
damp curls around her forehead. Soft floating feet kick up

the gold-belled filigree on her earrings. Tiny voices roar and crackle like fresh oiled corn in an earthen oven. They say that one day she will have a son and two daughters. Her son, they reveal, will depart early on to become a bird that lives in heaven. Her daughters, they say, will be born oceans apart. The first, Sugrah, will be soft, full of laughter, and contemplative, with unexpected heat igniting the corners of her mind. The second, Zafran, will be lean, of tight fists and squinting eyes, and a voice full of questions and arguments which will shake the logic from peoples' bones.

"Neither one is an easy road," one of the hazy eyed scribes whispers between folded hands which are bronze, small and penny hard.

"Tsk tsk, tsk." Pink as candy tongues strike and flash in agreement. The preciously sharp gates of a dozen milk teeth collide with the tip of lamenting pink.

"They'll misunderstand you at first Sonyah, but one day they'll begin to see that they cannot fly without accepting that it is you that primed their wings.

"Heaven lies at the feet of the mother," say the scribes, twisting the ends of their kurtas with star-like hands. "The Holy Prophet * spoke the truth. And one day your children will be noble enough to reach up and touch your feet. They will understand and embrace that part of you that has the power to request twin angels to open the silver locks of Paradise. As for now, take comfort in the fact that they will soon arrive in small, smooth, rosy brown packages. Soon they will need direction. You must become their North Star. Guide them. Soothe their wings and wait the storm out. It will be here before you know it. Brace yourself and your delicate bones, for the fury and confusion of daughters, my dear, will be core shattering clamor indeed."

The scribes wrap Sonyah's hair with a cord of jasmine entwined in soft wild grass. They tell her that to walk through the fire will not require the crystal scaffold of miracles. Nor will it require the carving of prayers on desert parched bone. The soles of her feet will not be burned because they will float above the fire. Held aloft by sheer force of belief. The belief that everything returns to its Creator. The belief that the Creator blesses both daughters and sons equally. The belief that in the days of Ignorance, revelation implored the faithless to stop burying their newborn daughters. The belief that daughters will some day become mothers. And as mothers, they will nourish tiny pods of ambling life so that one day they may ultimately walk with the dignity of oak and run like rain on stormy waters.

• ❖ •

Saturday morning. The kitchen. 8:05 a.m.

At the moment, my husband is walking the unpaved roads of his dreams. He lies rumpled up in peony and lace embroidered sheets that Mum'i had given us last week.

"For you, Zafran, and for my new son-in-law. I made them by hand."

"You made these by hand? It must have taken you a long time."

"Long enough to give me patience. Now, it is for you and my new son. It will give you patience. Keep you warm."

The sheets are actually cotton tablecloths that Mum'i had embroidered in preparation for her marriage to Ab'bu in 1961. Sitting on her mother's porch, overlooking the small hills by the Indian seacoast, Sonyah did not know that her youngest daughter's husband would be swaddled between her intricate floral threadwork. That a man, who bears the name of God's first man on Earth, would be dreaming of lakes filled with diamond-back turtles and fields of heather with her hand-crocheted lace under his chin, was something inconceivable; if not delightfully welcome.

Sonyah could never have known, as she and her nieces sat playing jacks with cowrie shells on the seashore, that a man from a two mile lake surrounded by broken canyon walls in the American West would lay dreaming in those same taut sheets.

This American man, my auburn haired Muslim with a canoe, will never know what a young Indian-Ethiopian woman was thinking as her delicate fingers threaded thin needles which pierced freshly washed and starched cotton in the endless heat of a tropical afternoon in Jailan.

While entranced on the island of sleep, he would be unaware that the tight knots of the deep fuschia flowers still remained as they were back then: stained with blood from too quick to embroider almond-colored fingers. A sturdy needle, as thin as a lone strand of silver hair, soaring through fabric as though it were the air itself, pricked a forefinger intent on completing the petals of lotus flowers in precise box stitches.

· ❖ ·

While dropping pieces of cinnamon bark and clove into a pot of boiling rice, Mum'i once asked me if I had ever tried to touch time.

"Time?" I asked as I placed a piece of clove in my mouth. For although I knew that the invisible worlds of time and space were, for her, like a constellation of friends, I was still in doubt of such a thing. "Mum'i," I said as I tasted the quick slide of clove spice, "I don't know what you mean."

"But you do. You do." Mum'i didn't look at me when she answered. Instead, she looked at the wall above the stove like she was peering through a window to the past. She smiled, closed her eyes and nodded her head like she was silently answering someone within that window. "Like air, I know that space and time are things we cannot touch," she said softly. "But if we long for those we miss, we can call them to us.

"Zafran," she said as she measured small pearly burs of basmati rice with her fist, "sometimes, when you think that your people aren't with you because you are far from them, or if they have passed, you are suddenly proven wrong. You may turn around one day and find their scent floating by your cheek and feel the brush of a familiar hand on your face. You'll go to the window because you hear your Nan'na's voice. You'll lift the curtain and find that it's your daughter sitting by a fence, braiding a doll's hair and singing a song you thought you had forgotten long ago."

I did not understand what she had said until I got married. But I suppose that I understand now. I understand very clearly. Even with its unending yards of black velvet, splinters of stars and cascading cosmic waterfalls, space is not a work of fiction; it is something real, a road leading to and from generations. Space and time become your guardians, your trusted friends, who take the four points of the sky in their hands as though it were a solid blue piece of silk. They become the hands of those you miss; draping the sky on your back and chest like warrior silk; groaning when those who come to hurt get a little too close; and urging you to push when intention alone does not emancipate desire.

This is the legacy of the women we all leave behind in the rush to forage for original hungers and livelihood. Taking from them what we can in youth, we sometimes forget that we have taken them into our hearts. For these women give and give without suspicion, suffocation or a second guess, and before you know it, you are back asking for more.

Yes, take the five dollars from my purse in the lamp table drawer.

Oh, you'll be home at eleven, a project with a friend, okay call from her house. Her parents will be there? Yes?

You'll be studying in London this summer, oh, and then France. You always did like to travel. We should've known since you were born with that black as a peppercorn freckle on the bottom of your foot. Oh, I must remind you to take your own towels, though. Remember, offer your Salat on time, and do not forget that Allah is with you at every step.

No, that's alright, Daddy and I can cancel the dinner.
No, it's no trouble at all. You just go ahead and work on your
thesis. Just tell me one thing: Will you need anything?

Sacrifices are made. Parents are put aside for a while.
Just long enough to go here, see about that, complete this and
make sure that is secured so that tomorrow will be easier.
After that, the years pass at light speed. Winters seem to get
colder and shelves become crowded with folders, envelopes,
and bills; the files and receipts of adult burdens. Suddenly,
there are two, three, four reflections in the bathroom mirror.
Then comes the shine and the kindness of keys.

Arrogance, arriving behind the tint and glare of a
confidence that only one's own salary can establish, becomes
the safety net under the cliffs of the empty places that hide
inside. The confidence is intoxicating. Sweet to the lick. It
signifies and convinces.

I believe it all. I tell myself that I stand tall. I can
stand alone. But I know one thing. It has taken its time, but
I can finally admit it to myself. When the world gets a little
too cold, when the corners I navigate get dangerously sharp,
at least there is one door that will always be open when the
need arises to go back for an hour, a day, an extended stay. I
embrace the welcome, security and refuge of old house keys.

Keys that were once held in the palm of a ninth grader's hand are now held in the palm of a woman. Dangling, clanging. A metal massage on fingertips eager to enter. Doors open. Parents smile.

I, the young woman who holds the keys, bears many titles in the outside world. Out there my name is followed by capital letters; mingled in the fancy rhymes of vocation; and roped to abbreviations, departments, categories and divisions. In the interior world, with its valley of carpets, curtains and kitchen tiles, I am simply known as daughter.

There are two pairs of feet which face me in this valley. Feet which once appeared so large and thunderous, now stand before me small, firm and weightless. They are buoyant, fleshy leaves fragile with age. Leaves that skim the cold top skin of the deep, still water lake that covers my eyes in the middle of the night. These feet can walk on water. Limber and pious to the bone. These feet float above an angry world; liberated by resolution and disclosure. Secrets have divulged their true missions. Misunderstandings have been clarified, understood and cleansed by the antiseptic of daylight. Longings, hopes and half-done dreams have been discussed, gently, as amongst friends over a modest dinner in which hushed laughter is more delicious than dessert.

These feet stand in a place that is no longer a way station between today's fury and tomorrow's intended escape. There is true comfort here. Acceptance and satisfaction have come to stay. There is no need to hide fears; there's no need to strive to be faceless. There is comfort here. Soothing without any questions. A visit without a desired thing, goal, or end. There's nothing to pick up, retrieve or take elsewhere. Not the extra something that's given at the end of a visit to take home; not that, not a thing, not a thing at all. It's the feet and hands themselves.

The older man who stands before me is no longer a statue with a frown. His eyes clearer, his brows a bit gray, heavy with thought, apology and consideration. His face seems older than it used to be when he lifted me over his shoulders to see the world, to reach crabapples with my hands. He smiles. It's the same smile that came out when I spelled something right; when I read my Surahs clearly, without hesitation; and when I rode that "too big for my child" horse without any help. He strokes my hand with the humbleness of one who saw the future coming and warned those in its way. He is my father.

The older woman covers a joyful face with her hands. Then her hands reach out to touch the palms of the one that once took refuge in the world inside her. Veins glow pink under tissue thin skin. Her smile is illuminated with the dignity of women who give without asking for anything in return. Strong, protective, compassionate; strengthened, tempered and gracefully stoic like the cycle before her.

The older woman, my mother, speaks volumes in her silence. The same silence that held the strength for three children and poetry written between bedtimes and rice porridge with a little saffron dissolving like orange-butter rain on top. Enough strength so that it could course and echo through the bones of her daughters like a last call from ship to shore. A warning to discourage the faint at heart and signal a "hold tight" for patience and mercy in preparation for the journey ahead. I look at my mother's face. Her eyes are heavy. She's been up since dawn for prayers.

Then and now my mother does not stand alone. There is an invisible army of strong shoulders and arms behind her. They are holding hands, leaning on one another, smiling, talking, singing, sobbing. Some are old and others young. They are familiar and unrecognizable. Mothers, grandmothers, aunts, cousins, sisters and friends whose footsteps etch soft, figure eights around the eyes. These are my women. My mothers through the ages who carry love like a shield as they march through centuries and shatter panes of gravity with their naked fists. Their love is mine; for this type of mother-love is as universal as it is personal. It is a table for two as it is a banquet for the many. They are calling me to their table. They are waving their strong, tanned arms. These women are calling me in quiet, without heavy breath or strain. They are calling me by my original name.

※

Tickets to Heaven

❖❖❖

"If a man has a daughter, brings her up well, feeds her properly,
and confers on her some of the bounties Allah has bestowed on him,
he has in her a guard to his right and a guard to his left—
all the way from the Fire to the Garden of Paradise."
- Sahih Hadith

*In old family photographs children always look like broken dolls
lodged in the pocket of a bitter wind. Their hair is a storm of
histories, glasses tilted like a broken vase on a fleshy plane and
clothes worn on distant memories of warm woolen blankets laid
atop cold blades of early fall grass.*

 *Raggedy, careless childhoods pass and the older girl whose
eyebrows you pulled for punishment, the girl whose pretty clothes
you secretly wore after she left for school, grows up, too. Parents,
who gave you the eye which held the promise of a cracking strap
after sunset, look at you now with steady heads anchored by patience
and eyes humbled in the security of their friendly orbits.*

• ❖ •

"Born oceans apart," my parents said. "One not like the other in any way. Two daughters are too much to handle some of the time and too much of a coolness for the eyes to want it any other way."

"We're one daughter short for a ticket to Paradise," my father joked with my mother. "Sonyah, do you think they'll let us in for just putting up with the stressful screams, temper tantrums and late night crying?"

"Insha'allah," Mum'i agreed nodding a head full of tight black curls softly twisted into a loose, friendly braid. She tickled the back of my neck to make me nod my head as well. "You would hope that our Creator would be so Merciful," Mum'i said while covering a laugh with her hands.

My father tugged my ear playfully and started to laugh. "Put in a good word for us at the gate, Zafran."

• ❖ •

My sister Sugrah and I were born twenty-two months apart after the quiet birth of a healthy boy whose delicate features and soft black curly hair favored our mother's side. A baby boy who would die in his sleep one day after birth. A "blue baby" whose gasps for oxygen in the middle of the night went unnoticed, ignored by hospital staff. (For a while, when I was young, I thought he died because he was sad—that's why they called him 'blue'. But my parents explained to my sister and I that he couldn't breath. He couldn't be saved in time.)

Oftentimes, I think that he is one of the reasons why my sister and I fought so hard with one another and the world. Defensive with one another but quick to rescue her sister from harm. Between us, the spoils and scrapes of childhood were shared on a level plane. Shame, hurt and agony triggered conference calls between our collective psyches. And if one messed up royally, or was somehow looped into bad company, the other felt equally guilty for permitting the harm to occur in the first place.

Don't look at my sister that way! What did you say about my sister? No, my sister isn't here right now. What do you want with her anyway? You're who? Spell your name slowly, so I can write it down. Who am I? Who am I! I am her sister, Zafran. Yes, I can spell it, Z-A-F-R-A-N. What does it mean? You want to know what it means? It means saffron. Oh, you don't know what saffron is? Don't they have it in New York? Go ask your mother.

Perpetual analysis of the world's motivations. And questions. There were always questions. Relentless in our quest for space, air and identity. Unwilling to let this world take our oxygen, we set out to inhale the world of books. With books in our hands, we would take greedy breaths. Thick books, colorful books, books above grade level.

· ❖ ·

"Excuse me little lady," the skinny librarian said to me as Sugrah and I sat on the plastic green chairs on the second floor of the Main Street Library. "Your sister there is much too young to actually understand that. That book has an Adult Classics label on it. You see, right... here."

A little confused at the comment, I pulled Sugrah's shirt and clung to *Beezus and Ramona*. She peaked above her pink plastic owl-eye frames, calmly placed the thick book with no pictures in it on the table, looked straight at the librarian and said, "Oh, I don't think you understand Miss. I like to read above grade-level. It's okay with our mom. Is that okay with you?"

Taken aback by my sister's comment, the librarian shrugged, pushed down her bifocals and quickly walked to the next table of eager, albeit underage, readers.

Mum'i usually picked us up at the library after an hour or so of dropping us off. She always had to check out Sugrah's books with her card since Adult Classics were off limits with ours. While leaving the building, she held our hands as we jumped down the shiny granite stairs of the library into the crowded intersection of Main Street and Kissena Boulevard.

As the first tenacious violets of the late afternoon started to glide atop the buildings, we found ourselves talking about the stories we were going to read that night. We three walked hand in hand. Two soft hands wearing complicated ruby rings holding two small ones knicked with pebbles and blushed with poster paints.

We stepped on the cracks of the sidewalk all the way home and played with doll size shadows which warped like stretched taffy with each move. Inspired by the fun-house quality of the shadows, I pressed Sugrah's braids up against her head like horns. "Horn girl, horn girl! You're the circus girl with horns!!!"

Sugrah suddenly stopped, contorted her nose and snapped her fingers in my eyes. She pulled one of the cat-face buttons on my sweater and pointed to Mum'i's shadow. It danced like a smoky genie over the peeling paint of the massive back walls of the Main Street movie theater. The shadow loomed higher than all the buildings on the street. We turned to look at one another behind Mum'i's back and nodded our heads in agreement. The shadows spoke the truth after all.

· ❖ ·

By six and seven, we knew the world was cruel. This we learned first-hand from the red-nosed man with greasy blond hair who drove the school bus. He said the bad things through yellow teeth. Some bad things we didn't understand. Words and noises explained to us by our neighbor Kamilya over broken Pringles during lunch time.

After we climbed the three large steps of the bus, we tried to steel ourselves. Every morning his comments were different. All I knew is that I felt the same each time. My cheeks got itchy hot; my throat felt like it was full of sand, and on top of that I thought I would vomit on my sister's brown suede school shoes.

The bus driver laughed under his breath. He said we smelled.

As we passed him, he held his nose between cracked yellow fingers and yelled "Pee-U" to the children seated in the bus.

"Don't stink up the bus now girls," he said between laughs. "Hey girls, where's the other half of the litter this morning?" Words said with the cavalier confidence of one whose power is sealed by height and weight alone. Children can't fight a man with the baffling girth of ignorance.

I was always first to cry after we got to our seats.

"Zafran, shut up," my sister commanded. "Do you want him to think he's smarter than us?"

"No," I said between hiccups and sobs. "No, no. I don't want that."

"Okay, then be quiet. Here, read your book."

In the ripped sticky seat of a public school bus, my sister helped me to understand that one death, that of a baby boy with smooth pink palms by strangers' negligence, was enough grief for our family. She made sure I understood that as her nails made slender half moons on the flesh of my right hand. As my tears fell on her feverish grip, she knew that I'd understood, and that I'd try to be strong.

"Always remember that," she said. "It won't happen again if I can help it."

Squeezing the book in my hand, I looked out through the window to see early shoppers on Main Street pushing grocery carts and baby carriages.

As the cover of my book slowly dampened with salty tears, the binding puckered to shape my sweaty grip. My bladder suddenly gave in, immediately pushing down to fill my belly with stinging pain. I pushed the book against my stomach. Maybe it would ward off the pain for a while.

Sugrah sat in a dignified deep-freeze. I didn't hear a word or a breath. She didn't even blink. She did not look at me. Turning her head to the back of the bus, she stared back at the children staring at us. Turning back around, she began to rifle through overstuffed jacket pockets. After a minute or so, she turned to me. She untangled a dusty tissue from three silver jacks, shook it out like a wet sock and pressed it in my hand. Taking the book from my hands, she placed it back in her school bag and got back to the business of sweeping the day's misery from under our dangling feet.

• ❖ •

Girls, our parents taught us, could do anything in the world. Yes, the world was cruel. Yes, it was full of nasty, mean and morally questionable things done by the shattered minds of a heartbroken people. Yes, all these things were there they said, but so too were spring flowers and butterflies at Queens Botanical Garden, long car trips to the seashore and Bear Mountain, and miracles that we had yet to experience.

There were dark things in this life, but we were told to fight to see the other side.

"Go and see what America has to offer," my father said, waving a black fountain pen as fat as a cigar in our faces.

For both Sugrah and I, our father was a man of towering intelligence and sharp as steel wit. A man whose leather slippers burned us so hard in punishment that it made us consider crawling back into our mother's womb—head first. But we knew we'd be yanked out by a man who fought too long and hard in this country to let his daughters get lost so easily. His daughters would not be that weak. He had promised to leave our apartment in his pajamas in the dark of night, lose a limb and a portion of his mind to make sure of it. He would not to allow his children to drown and disappear in this country. That was not something he could accept, let alone fathom.

"I am trying to make you girls into fighters," he said when he waxed reflective (which was always). "Fighters don't cry at the drop of a hat. They don't let people tell them what they can or cannot be. If you need my blood, your mother's blood you can have it. Allah gave us enough to share. Use your feet. Use your minds. Keep your heart safe, and don't take good for granted. You're not stupid children. We love you with our hearts, your mother and I. You won't understand now. Not now. The older one, she's a poet, a writer, a trouble maker with a guilty conscience. The younger one, she's thin-skinned, sensitive, always finds the need to run. She will be a traveler I suppose, an arguer—that I'm sure of. She talks much too loud for her age. That will save her, probably. People will close their ears while she moves ahead. These are my children. My two children. The coolness of my eyes. *Alhamdolillah.*"

Arriving in America in the early Sixties, my father worked as a teacher and earned two Masters degrees at night. Having taught in three countries where teachers were respected like one's parents, he entered his first New York City classroom to realize that things were going to be different in Manhattan. After working in five schools in two years, two of which were closed due to "negative student initiative," he sent for his family.

A one bedroom apartment in Queens (in a building with an actual elevator that I first took to be *our apartment* by mistake), new American-style clothes, solid oak tables and dressers, clean cotton sheets from S. Klein's department store, two Mary Jane dolls and three boxes of Schraft's chocolates with blue plaid bows, were all ready for his wife and two daughters.

The first night in our new apartment, I walked around endlessly from living room, to kitchen, to bedroom just feeling the walls. Clean, cold, white walls. Sugrah and I jumped on our new beds over and over until our parents could bear it no more. They were in the living room so we decided to take liberties just like true Americans would. So we jumped and jumped until the mattress flattened out under our feet like a spongy thin, quilted pancake. By the time our parents walked in the room, I had managed to knock the headboard off with an overeager kick to express my happiness over my new home.

My sister and I played hide and seek in the closets. We were amazed at how many clothes they could hold. We pressed our faces against our father's coats, dress slacks and dress shirts and put our feet into our mother's size 8 wedge-heeled espadrilles. We laughed while holding new dresses under our chins in front of a warped mirror that was as big as we were and wider than both of us put together. We stood with our new dresses in our hands and tried to speak like the Americans we saw on the first floor of the building when we walked in. Moving our mouths in slow motion, we attempted to make stylish conversation in our new American repertoire,

"Hello, how are you, my name is...Yes, it is a buu-tee-ful day, isn't it...Oh yes, this is my sister..."

This was going to be our home. Permanently. The thought was a bit scary, but at the same time it was a relief. We were going to live here, in America. We were going to make American friends and sit in colorful classrooms with tall, pretty teachers that looked like the stewardesses on Pan Am.

"You will both have opportunities that your Mum'i and I never had. But you must always remember one thing: achieve what you want, but never forget who you are." These were the words my father doled out in deep bass tones at the end of each meal. These were the words I saw Sugrah saying to the mirror while combing her hair at night.

• ❖ •

When we offered our Maghrib prayer together, my father always asked me or my sister to do the closing du'a. My sister, pushed to the edge of annoyance by elbow knocking and requests to "please let me do it , please, please," always gave in. So by default, by sheer and utter greed, it was up to me to say the closing prayer.

I picked at the limp, golden tassels tied to the ends of the prayer rug waiting for my moment. This was the part I always waited for. My veins filled with the rush of anticipation that in a few short moments I would talk to Allah alone. I, upon this worn blue velour rug made in Kashmir, would have the Ear of God. My Creator, my Benefactor. He of the generous, light drenched Hands would listen to a child who lived in apartment 6G. This was staggering. This was why I liked being Muslim.

My friends said I was lucky to be able to talk to God all by myself. They asked if I could take Him some requests.

"Can you ask him about my sister's diary?" asked Leigh as he peeled the ends of a bologna sandwich.

"Hey, can you try to find out where Noah's Ark really is?" asked Michele.

"Uh, can you ask him to take the lump out from my hamster's throat?" requested Charles.

"No," I responded, diplomatically nodding my head and slapping my hands in disgust of such a thought. I had the Ear of Allah, but I wasn't, after all, an intermediary. I advised them to talk to Him by themselves. Alone.

"Just ask Him," I said. "But remember to ask nicely, though. And remember to speak clearly, loudly...and don't ask for too much because that's too greedy. He's busy you know. He's trying to make everyone happy. Okay?"

The part of Salat I liked the best was when I cupped my hands, squinted one eye in concentration, and looked up to talk to Allah. The harder the squint, the better the signal, the sharper the frequency of transmission. Eyes tight, tight,

tight. The tighter the eyes, the quicker the travel time of the request, I figured.

"Insha'allah, begin Zafran," my father encouraged softly.

The closing prayer was the same each time: a short, rapid list of love, health and blessings to all— especially to those sick and in need. Tacked on to the end were those special requests.

"Oh Allah, please help Charles get over the chicken pox, and help Sugrah get first place in the story-telling contest. Oh Allah, make my parents buy me a German Shepherd, a cat maybe, or even some fish. And help me to pass that math test on Monday."

My parents spirituality, their uncompromising love of Allah, made me feel like things would be safe for us. For how could parents who prayed five times a day, fed the hungry and fasted for one whole month throughout the year do anything or say anything to little girls who had the power to talk to Allah all by themselves?

2-205

❖❖❖

Mrs. Silverstein was my second grade teacher. She was the blue haired queen of the second floor. The green eyeshadowed matron of innocent six year olds poised on the precipice of a new world. Every night of my second grade life hinged on the fear that I would have to take my seat in row 2 seat 2 and watch the frosted pink lips of my large hipped teacher mouth out phrases, words, numbers and dates in scary slow motion so that those new to *"our* country" could understand.

For a child who had recently immigrated from a country where primary schools were *always* built on ground level, a child who hadn't had enough time to learn to trust her environment, life was scary enough without having to trudge back to a room guarded by the gaze of a woman who announced freely that doom resided in the dense blood of her red marker pen.

Every morning, I faced the prospect of returning to a room full of felt numbers, flag pledging and bathroom visits in pairs.

The maze of hallways on the second floor of PS 20 were purely frightening. At any turn, you could find yourself face to face with another pair of disoriented second graders who, like you and your "bathroom buddy", had found themselves lost while using the pass. If you were truly unlucky, you would find yourself at the mercy of tall third or fourth graders who called you a "baby bumper" before they knocked you into a wall. If there existed the fate of something worse, it could probably have been traced back to the confines of room 2-205. This was the place where the fears of my six year-old mind began *and* ended.

· ❖ ·

Every night after I finished my homework, when the reality of returning to room 2-205 crept up in my mind, the fear would start again. That was one thing I had no control over.

The things that I did have control over were sheets of crisp, lined paper, sharpened pencils and tightly-bound black and white notebooks. All these things brought me joy, and when I found a pink eraser on my father's desk one day, it just made everything magical. If I made a mistake, it rubbed clean off. Just blow on the paper a little and everything could be scrubbed brand new. Then the paper was clean and ready. With the pink eraser, there was always a second chance for straight etched *T*'s, swirling *S*'s and rapid *O*'s.

After the last page of homework, just after Mary and Dick took the last skip around their yard, the fear planted itself in my head. I was knotted in sweaty sleep until the morning. I smelled the classroom in my dreams and felt the swift pummel of Mrs. Silverstein's fist on my desk if any spelling errors should arise.

In the morning I washed my face with hard splashes of cold water. Like a soldier, I thought. I would freeze the skin on my face and deal with the agony of the day.

Mum'i would always be smiling and issuing advice for the day as I wiped the sleep from my eyes at 7:15 a.m. She sweetly hollered as she peeked at me from the kitchen, "Zafran, fix that collar and put some socks on! Come here so I can pin the hair away from your face. Zafran! Remember to say Bismillah before you eat."

While I ate my corn flakes, she came over to kiss the side of my head, say three prayers and then blow softly on my face. The woolly nubs of her cardigan brushed my cheek, embracing me in the scent of sandalwood: the perfume of safety and strong women who promised to raise even stronger daughters.

My mother was the sixth child in a family of seven. She was named after a constellation of seven stars, moved with my father to three countries and spoke five languages. While cooking four dishes at a time, she could still find the time to comb my hair, slide in two hair pins and find the missing plastic sheep from the Fisher-Price Farm Family.

She was all these things as well as a woman of beauty and kindness who always packed the tomatoes separately, so the bread would not get mushy. She was the doctor of lunch distress who cured the morning blahs by wrapping toffee and cake in floral paper napkins. They would be waiting in the corner of my lunch box providing five minutes of sweet relief in a lunchroom sagging from the misery and stench of cold bologna and spilt milk.

After leaving my mother's gentle hands, I had to find the strength to battle the Dragon Lady of room 2-205. Mum'i didn't know that dragons awaited me in PS 20. I never told her.

"School is good for little girls. You both should be thankful that you have a school to go to," was what Mum'i said in her melodious voice before she kissed Sugrah and I good-bye at All Grades morning line-up in the school yard.

Morning line-up was first call to the lunch-box army. The portly assistant principal, Mr. Kaufman, blew his whistle to signal ranks of three and a half foot soldiers, outfitted in Garanimals and Health-Tex separates, to march slowly, methodically to their designated rooms. Each infantry followed a bouffant haired drill sergeant armed with a pocket book and silver necklace of twenty-nine keys. Clanging keys dangled over hearts pierced like a sieve to mark thirty-four long years with short people of many requests.

After following Mrs. Silverstein's double-knit hem to the confines of room 2-205, there would be a another line-up to deposit lunch box, coat and school-bag inside the closet.

The closet was opened by a willowy sixth grade monitor, named Lisa, who was assigned to Mrs. Silverstein for the year. Among her other duties were to get a "sugar no creme" coffee for our teacher from the teachers' lounge and bring us down to lunch.

Lisa always did the same thing after lunch. She led our class into the middle of the school yard and separated us into dodgeball teams. Even if we didn't want to play dodgeball, we were forced to comply. Lisa was taller than any of us, and she was *the monitor*. She even had a green and yellow badge that said Service Squad. What Lisa wanted, Lisa got. As she swung her waist length blond hair to the side, and adjusted the cuffs on her hip hugging bell-bottoms, she stuck a wad of gum on the back of her hand and pointed to the yellow line on the ground. That meant we had to line up while she separated us into specific teams. If there was a protester or two, a couple of kids who questioned their team assignment, they were immediately served a red demerit card and forced to stand with their faces against the chain-link fence until the end of recess.

Lisa, with her polished skills of sorting (probably acquired by way of South Africa or Mississippi), always divided the two teams according to the Lisa Principle. According to this principle, all the cutesy boys and pretty girls were placed on Team A. And all the non-white and recently immigrated children were placed on Team B. If anyone on Team B touched Lisa at any point during the game, she would squeal "Yuck, foreigner cooties." This would incite Team A members to follow her lead in stereo.

Lisa made sure there was no horsing around while we hung our coats on metal hooks which protruded like gunmetal question marks from the recesses of the closet. Mrs. Silverstein put her in charge while she went to her personal closet at the back of the room to change her shoes. This happened every day like clockwork. Third graders who had her last year told stories about her closet at lunch time. Mrs. Silverstein's closet became the last frontier, a place of mystery and unmentionable amazement, a Pandora's box of secrets which entranced the observer with a sharp whiff of Ben-Gay ointment.

The students who were on the back of the closet hang-up line always peered inside Mrs. Silverstein's closet to see which shoes would be stalking up the aisles for the day. Inside her closet lay a neat shelf of shoes, a mirror and a large photograph of her with a three happy looking kids who looked just like her.

As she locked her closet with one of the twenty-nine keys around her neck, Mrs. Silverstein placed the day's pair next to her neat desk by the window. She carefully sat down, adjusted the pleats of her skirt, briskly reprimanded her aching knees and then slipped off the rubber soled shoes to reveal stubby, soft pink toes that looked like a family of hard boiled eggs.

For an old lady who spent most of her time with those who hadn't even mastered the skill of fine motor coordination, Mrs. Silverstein was still very particular with the shape, style and color of her shoes. There were always little bows or large rhinestones on the back of brightly colored, well polished pumps.

The shoes designated the day's turn of events. Open toes meant art in the afternoon. Double straps meant some sorry child would be called to the board for a math problem which would inevitably result in the wrong answer. Stacked black heels always meant a child would vomit after a spelling test; but red high heels were a flag in the wind. Red heels were cause for celebration. They signaled that at the end of the day one lucky row would get to pick prizes from the Scholastic Books grab bag.

There was no need for fortunes resting on the tiny faces of tea leaves. We, the crayon bearing masses of 2-205, always received the daily horoscope, squished and screaming, from inside Mrs. Silverstein's pumps.

· ❖ ·

After gongs signaling the end of first hour, the class was led down to the music room for recorder lessons. Recorders, fake plastic flutes for the safety-scissors population, were dependable, easy and generous with immediate gratification. They gave us meaning even though we were pinched if we played the wrong note.

Going down to the music room always meant being greeted by a bob-haired teacher named Mrs. Heleno. A woman who never seemed to blink and perpetually picked lint off her clingy Quiana wrap-dresses. She was the type of teacher whose sharply outlined lips gave credence to the rumor that there were people on this planet who actually did eat children for breakfast.

The rumors were there, but the worst we were forced to endure was maybe a nasty pinch or two if we were off-key for "Three Blind Mice."

Mrs. Heleno was a woman for whom music was something pathological. It was a thing that consumed oneself—a thing to suffer for and make others suffer for as well. Before each lesson, she would clear her throat and with an air of pride deliver Words Of Meaning in her lilting First Lady of MGM via the Sorbonne accent.

"I used to play weez zah London Symphony and seeng weez zah Paris Opera. But ven I came to zees country, I decided I vaz going to help leetle cheeldren. You too can become great person of museek like your teejher."

We couldn't disappoint a woman of such experience and passion. We were going to play those saliva sprayed recorders, and we were going to play them well.

"Cheeldren, if you punish the museek, then you, too, must be punished."

If we played incorrectly, we were pinched. Some of us wore our tiny black and blues like battle scars. We had suffered for the music, and for Mrs. Heleno, that was noble suffering, indeed.

The end of recorder lessons would be followed with American Folk Songs Unit Four. We had graduated from "She'll Be Coming Around The Mountain" to the epic "This Land is Your Land."

It was only during the squeaky voiced singing of these songs that America would come alive. It was only during these songs that my classmates and I actually sang at the top of our lungs. The fear of the day would somehow dissolve for a three minute reverie of redwood forests, purple mountains and darling Clementine.

We looked at one another, backs straight, hands locked at our waists and smiled. We looked at Mrs. Heleno's bob swaying, her fingers pounding with furious intensity at her Board of Education piano and felt that things were not all that bad after all. Our voices, within the wood floored music room of a public elementary school in Queens, sang high. For that moment, our lungs were strengthened with something small and mighty that mattered.

It was usually at this point that Mrs. Silverstein showed up. Her shoes announced her arrival. She stood nodding her head and smiling. Smiling? Smiling at us with a face glowing under a fresh dusting of powder. She stood, feet firmly stationed nine inches apart, batting ancient eyelashes covered in the tar of mascara petrified since 1953. The weight on her lids alone could have most certainly caused blindness. Yet, she saw us clear enough to put a smile on her face. She looked at us with surprised doe eyes full of hope and expectation. As though she had accidentally come upon twenty-four of her best friends while purchasing discounted nylons in the hosiery section of Gertz department store on Roosevelt Avenue.

When we finished our song, Mrs. Silverstein clapped along with all of us. She even joined Mrs. Heleno in a flurry of "Bravos".

As she walked to the front of the room, she tapped me and each person in row five on the shoulder. "Very nice, children. Very nice."

She smelled like Ponds cold cream and when she came closer, I saw that her hands and arms were covered with light brown spots. Spots which moved with the sudden shift of the fragile skeleton they clung to. Spots just like my Nan'na's.

She could be somebody's grandma I thought. And if she could be somebody's grandma, she most certainly was somebody's mother. I pictured her powdered face next to her grandchild's. I pictured her putting a warm plate of eggs and toast in front of her children.

A six year old philosophized about teachers actually being people and having real families. That a teacher could have a life outside of class 2-205 and sit with an actual family outside the red brick walls of PS 20 was something truly bizarre.

Second graders should be the nation's philosopher laureates. Their experience in the world at the bright old age of six or seven proves that even the most primitive of philosophies arises from the Original Truth. Namely, that human suffering always occurs as a result of mean teachers and cheap parents. And if a teacher could actually be nice, then there was always room to celebrate and abrogate the Original Truth—even it was only half-way.

While Mrs. Silverstein and Mrs. Heleno exchanged gossip and class behavior notes before the twin gongs signaling third hour, I thought about my Nan'na who always took her chai in a garden of wild grass and jasmine three oceans away. A Nan'na whose name meant leader of women. An aging spirit who rose before dawn for her morning prayers and counted tasbee beads with fingers embroidered in black henna.

With all her fiery breath, expert frigidity and favoritism, Mrs. Silverstein was only human after all. Had I been born in Queens to an American family named Silverstein,

I could very well be calling her grandma and speaking with a weird American accent to some cousin named David.

Although the thought had a frightening ring to it, it actually comforted me in a way. I still hated her for making me feel the seizing fear each night but now she was no longer a dragon lady. She was different. She was human and had spots on her hands just like my Nan'na.

Monster's Request

❖❖❖

" Have We not lifted up your heart,
and relieved you of your burden,
which weighed down your back?
And have We not given you high renown?
With hardship comes ease.
Indeed, with hardship comes ease."
- Qur'an 94:1-6

The first light after Fajr cools the soul with a brightness that washes you clean from afar. This piece of curative sky and light is thrown your way by the favor of your Creator. Nothing else has this beauty. It feels as though the world is set ablaze for your amusement only. It is fluid in its warmth, and salat becomes a covering for your soul. "Protect me from the ugliness of unkind people, save me from the savagery of the unkind word," you say.

Small requests to a Being who is bountiful in His response. He only asks that you ask so that He may provide and procure. And you have asked with a gentle voice; a whisper almost. But to the Almighty, this whisper tears through the limitless ink-blue and lavender post dawn sky and falls right into His Merciful Hands.

• ❖ •

The morning was filled with bountiful breezes and reticent light. It was a morning like those balmy days spent at the seashore. The air is charged, light and the ensuing feelings that arise are just as sweet and lilting.

Within this morning, Sugrah carried her burdensome Monster. She could not shake it off for the last two days. It wasn't leaving anytime soon and gave her the feeling that it would suck all her strength, patience and compassion like a blood thirsty parasite. She had the feeling that the coming days would become an onerous eternity. The triumvirate would succeed again: Knotted stomach, throat and shoulders ready to claim her as their one and only plaything.

That familiar rod of painful nervousness and tension wrapped itself throughout her spinal column: unsolicited sadistic metallurgy. There was no release in sight. No rescue or uncoiling. There was no hand smoothing down the pierced raw consciousness of a person-that-was and who just wanted-to-be once again.

Another try. Another chance at flight. These things were not shimmering like golden keys in the horizon. The door was locked. Airtight.

Sugrah went to the ocean after fajr and had a wonderful time. She felt the Monster's presence but when her husband is around it seems to feign good behavior, at least some of the time. This was not one of those times. When she comes home, it arrives. Full blast, mouth on fire and ready to inhale her, head first. She tries to control it but when it is challenged, when she tries to keep from becoming fallen prey, it takes her soul and crushes it into compact, thorny metal discs and shoves them between her neck and spine.

· ❖ ·

When they were children, Sugrah told her sister how the pain got worse at night. Right before they went to sleep is when it became unbearable. From under a floral-print comforter, she would try to explain. "I feel like I'm being crushed from within, like the floor will disappear, and I won't be able to climb out from under it."

Her sister, Zafran, a second grader at the time, would bring her whatever she could find in the medicine cabinet above the toilet. Sometimes Bayer, sometimes sweet cherry cough syrup. Other times, she would reach to the top shelf and bring her menstrual cramp medicine. Little hands full of offerings from the pharmacy in the bathroom. Sugrah took what her sister brought on the top of cold palms in the middle of the night.

"Don't chew them," Zafran said. "They're not Cheerios." She would give Sugrah a piece of chocolate to fight the taste of chalky, crunched up aspirin. Other times it was a quick gulp of Tang or Nestle's Quick. As a child, pain gave her no choice but to give in. She took what was available from an unlicensed seven year old doctor in blue flannel pajamas with fuzzy feet.

Real doctors, the ones at the hospital, told her parents it was just growing pains. She told them about the headaches and needle sized gray ghosts that she felt near her in the dark. They told her to stop watching scary movies and to go to sleep an hour earlier. "Eat better," they said. "Oh, it's just her age. Just cut out all those cheese doodles before bedtime, and she'll be fine."

Her parents knew it was not a phase, and it was not a matter of diet. It was not as simple as that. For their child, their daughter who started to read at the age of four, the diagnosis could not be that simple. This was not a case of a careless diet or out of control hormones. They held her tight and stroked her damp forehead when she screamed in the middle of the night.

Zafran kept an eye on her, too. If Sugrah started to talk about gray needles in the middle of assembly, Zafran would run to the school pay phone, and on tip-toes reach up to call their father to take them home. "It's happening again," she said in whispers. "Its happening. Come soon, Daddy. Please."

But at night, things just got worse. There would be ten, twenty gray needles and hot, stinging invisible things poking her skin. She couldn't describe it sometimes. Lying awake at night, having no name for her suffering, she always felt like she was building her own prison. Distilling shapes from the shadows cast on the bedroom ceiling, she swallowed quickly and twisted the sheets in her hand. Two knots for hope. One more knot for mercy.

It was tortuous for Zafran when she heard her sister cry in the dark because of an evil without a face that lurked in her head and throat. An evil without a name that took liberties to visit without name, appointment or identification.

The Monster told Sugrah she was slow, dumber than the other children. It made fun of her accent, pushing its needles in her side when she was called on to read aloud in class. It laughed at her with her classmates all through school. Nowadays, it stared at her with unblinking eyes and stone frowns just like her colleagues did at the office when she adjusted her hijab during meetings and asked that alcohol not be ordered when she ate out with them. She tried not to listen to it. She tried not to give in. Once, she had looked at it in the eye and ordered it to stop, but when she went to work the next day, there it was, sitting on her chair and telling her she was stupid; that her scarf and loose dresses made her look ugly. After that, the headaches became more painful and the needles became stronger—relentless.

It was because of her childhood memories of her sister's desire to help, that Sugrah decided she had to make a small request. A final invocation for sanity. She asked Him, the One Zafran fought tooth and nail to make requests to on her blue Salat rug, to evict this thing. This tenacious, brutal thing whose constant consumption of little girl hearts provided mood energy for madness. The one who had been her cut-throat, uninvited whispering companion since she was eleven. She wanted one thing: To take this thing and move it someplace outside herself; to banish it from her soul. To rid herself of this one-sided sanity sucking friendship that made her use the pass at least six times a day in junior high. It was the one that made her pull at the roots of her hair in the girls bathroom until the physical hurt helped her to forget what lay in wait inside.

She clasped her hands in prayer. She read what she could remember of the du'as she was taught. With His help she tried to fight the Monster, but her own will was a collection of shards which were too fragile, too easily overwhelmed. She lost the battle at first, but she was still standing. There was a chance. She had to believe. Believe in the One Who said, "Walk to Me, and I'll come to you at speed."

• ❖ •

Inside her parents' apartment the world started to melt. She remembered that five minutes ago, she walked in a bent-up shadow of a person. As she sat there, listening to their beautiful voices, engulfed in their exponential love, the Monster stepped out from her body. Its bloody hands and feet emerged slowly;

its skin wrinkled from the pickling fight of eighteen years. Her mother was holding her in her arms just as she had held her when Zafran was eight and had run to the living room to announce, for the third time that day, that she thought Sugrah was dying.

Sugrah watched the Monster disappear as it stepped out through the window and slid down the trunk of the tree outside the living room window. Just like that, just that swiftly. In a matter of seconds it had fled. She felt as if a thorny ball had been soothed out of tired skin and a once familiar burden had been carefully dislodged, moved and cast from the hinges of her skull.

She remembered looking at her parents' faces, feeling cradled halfway between the friendly brightness of natural light and folded within the waves of a warm fresh water sea. While she focused on their eyes, she saw the struggle of eighteen years. They had pulled it from her and sucked the Monster dry. She tried to remember if they had opened the window.

"How dare you hurt our daughter," their eyes yelled and collided with the dense air of Monster leavings. "Did you really think we would let you take her. Have you no understanding of a mother's love, of a father's grief?"

She felt as though she had emerged from water. She was fed. Hunger vanquished by the soothing of a fragile heart.

Echoes of banging stones ticked softly in her arms. Love, in her shameless blue-gold package, emanated from her parents' hearts like a sweetly scented palm leaf moving over the length of her face and shoulders to finally embrace her arms.

Their love, and His love, pulled her back to Earth. She climbed, one limb at a time, back inside herself. They had evicted the Monster and enabled her to claim her body and mind once again. She had been called back to Earth by love alone. And though their hands were not upon her, she still felt like she was being rocked. Gently and with loving tenacity she was being rocked. It went on for what seemed like an endless wave and a millisecond all at the same time.

She remembered that He said, "Ask me, for I love to give. Walk to Me and I'll run to you...A door will shut and thousands will open in its place."

A small door, or was it a gaping window, had opened. He said it was her decision alone whether to walk in or wait. Her parents gave each other knowing looks. They knew, even if she did not, that it was time. How could they not know. Wasn't their blood in her veins? Wasn't her breath in theirs?

Finally, Sugrah pushed herself up from the sofa, took five small steps and was received with the strength of mighty words and carried further by the softness of mighty winds.

Her parents and husband watched her with kind eyes. They smiled, wanting to say something, wanting to reach out their hands. But they knew it was up to Sugrah. They said nothing, but she felt the embrace of their confidence; the unyielding support of familiar bones. Their belief in the One that Healed shot under her feet; a current of warm light; a bridge leading her out of an enervating struggle to the fresh air of resolve. Nothing seemed cloudy. Nothing seemed obscured in the shadows of self-doubt. Everything was clear. Hope had re-entered her veins.

There were no more needles stinging at Sugrah's side. No gray ghosts stood whispering past mistakes and signaling false signs. She was tired, exhausted by the fulfilling agony of extraction. She saw a place outside herself, a place where her people, her parents, were her pillars. She placed the weight of eighteen years in His hands. Those Hands, once forgotten in a cloud of agony and confusion, were now familiar again. They were full of compassionate reminders. They had held her up when she, herself, had forgotten that she had the power to stand.

Coverings

❖❖❖

" And among His signs is this:
He creates for you mates from among yourselves,
so that you may dwell in tranquillity with them,
and He engenders love and tenderness between you:
in this, behold,
there are Signs for those who reflect."
- Qur'an 30:21

People say that you have to straighten out all your problems with your parents before you have your own kids. If you don't, then they'll probably end up having the same problems that you had as a child.

I can never understand what went wrong between my parents. I think about it a lot, and you'd probably think I'd have it all figured out by now. But I suppose that's a lot like dropping a glass vase and expecting the surface to be just as smooth and perfect after the breaking. In reality, you end up collecting a thousand shards: sharp puzzle pieces that prick and cut until you glue everything back together. It takes time, and the final product is still a little defective, a little off-kilter.

The pieces just don't fit right because with fifteen Band-Aids on your fingers, you just can't glue all that well.

· ❖ ·

Princess Kamilya is what Daddy called me when I was little. I used to look around. Where? Where's the princess? There's no princess here. This is when my childhood would get lodged like a tangled piece of chickenwire inside my windpipe. Wrung out by my pain, I'd rush to my room, shut the door, squat on the floor and hold my head between my bony knees.

But one thing is for sure, no one could say that Kamilya was a bad girl. The one and only thing that I could always be caught with is the slick residue of goodness on my hands.

There were no courtiers bearing gifts or a joyful king and queen to notice my goodness. I had a private arsenal which I appreciated for myself—in secret. A stockpile of good deeds, certificates and straight A's shoved into the recesses of my desk (I'd probably be called conceited if they were displayed in public). I was coated with Model Minority Teflon. Guarded from filmy accusations, bad statistics, bad grades and bad grammar. Nothing could stick to a girl who placed first in the fifth grade District 25 Spelling Bee.

· ❖ ·

Our castle was in Queens, New York. A khaki colored building six stories high across the street from a Chinese vegetable market and around the corner from a bodega with a rusty mustard awning. You could see the shiny steel World's Fair Globe from our fire escape window. And on certain days, when the sun was just right, the Twin Towers poked through the Globe like a massive glass and cement peace sign pointing to the heavens.

On this fairy tale island, sandwiched half-way between Main Street and College Point Boulevard, I achieved on my own what other kids only dreamed about. I was student of the month. I was the token immigrant achiever with teachers who extolled the virtues of my "disciplined" study habits and complimented my "friendly parents" who always sent deep dishes of rice and roasted meat to International Day assembly.

It was during special assemblies that I peeked through clumpy bangs, which always obscured my eyes, to accept an award with the politeness expected of "those children who have recently arrived on *our shores.*"

I grinded my teeth under my smile when my teachers complimented me in class. I practiced that smile at home before the mirror. It was perfect, like the smile of those kids in the cereal commercials. All that was left was lifting a spoon to my mouth and saying "Yummy" with the integrity of a politician. Instead of cereal, I had delicious certificates carefully lettered in the graceful swirls of calligraphy.

From my seat in the auditorium, I saw the teacher mouth my name in slow motion as she waved the award like a flag in the center of the stage. The room suddenly became hollow, like the ceremony was taking place inside a conk shell. I couldn't see the kids sitting in my row. They became a blur of plaid pants, turtlenecks and hair bows. All I saw was the teacher's hand holding a fancy piece of paper with my name on it.

My feet hit the floor of the auditorium like they were made of iron. As I trudged down the aisle I began to prepare. And then it was time. It was easy since I practiced beforehand. Although there was no signifying drum roll, no countdown of 3, 2, 1, the smile instinctively knew when to make its appearance. Pulled from the dark, throbbing core of my throat like a frightened bunny from a top hat, it made an appearance, quickly, under flaring nostrils which searched for extra oxygen. After the ceremony was over, I'd run to the bathroom to spit the violent taste of embarrassment and bitter acquiescence from my mouth. For a ten year old who still carried a Green Card, the momentary goodness of a prize was a shield, a deflector of one's true needs. It was not, after all, a healer.

• ❖ •

Every day after school, I ran home to see if my goodness made me grow or something. Then realizing I was home and facing the fact that I did not have a love to call my own, I felt as though I was shrinking with each moment. The windows became gaping blocks of brightness that had the power to swallow me whole. The walls were too clean, too spare and the whole house smelled of fetid emotions and thick-skinned reticence.

There were fragrant pots on the stove every afternoon, and each time I peeked in I saw myself floating in the gravy or pinned limply upon a bone with oozing marrow.

I took my dish to my room and sat in front of the TV while the Brady kids tramped and whined throughout their thirty room house in bell bottoms and polyester shirts. They were always throwing fits about braces, prom dresses, trading stamps, and wanting their own room. At least their parents loved each other, or put on a good act, I thought.

My neighbor, Zafran, said somebody should put bugs down one of Cindy Brady's frilly Shirley Temple dresses. "Put the straw haired girl though some real pain. Put her out of her misery," she said while crunching unpeeled carrots.

Zafran's sister, Sugrah, would always disagree. "Come on Zafran and Kamilya. Leave them alone. They're just kids. Even if they do have thirty rooms in their house, it doesn't mean they're all that happy ."

I liked them both. They seemed to understand what I couldn't actually say out loud. We usually sat together at lunch. Theirs was the company I liked. They also had a

brother like mine. Their brother had gone, too. We talked
about our brothers a lot. Zafran always said that she saw
them both in her dreams. She said she asked about them in
her prayers.

"They're both in heaven, " she reported back to us as
though she spoke to Allah directly. Like she had a private
line or something. "I've seen them; they're happy. They have
lots of nice things to eat and wear. They're clean and pretty,
too. He held them up in His Hands to show me. 'See Zafran;
they're fine', He said just like He always speaks. All nice and
hushed and everything. Like He's saying something that only
I should hear. But I can tell you both, too. He said it was
okay, you know, to tell you both. I said that we were their
sisters. We just wanted to know if they were okay and all. If
they needed anything extra."

· ❖ ·

Mommy always came in my room while I was eating to ask if
I wanted seconds. "Have some more rice, a little more chicken.
They say that skinny girls get sick quicker than those who
have healthy appetites."

As if good nutrition was all I had to worry about in
this cruel and moody world. A world that was ready to slap
me with both hands and feet. A duplicitous world which
would back off for a day or two while it gathered the strength

to rise up again as though I were its chosen enemy. That's when I'd feel a stroke or two. A certificate, an award with shiny gold and silver star stickers would be distilled by good behavior. Then quickly, as I walked back to my assigned seat, I felt a swift slap on my back; quick and hard, razor sharp like the wind. Cold hands clutched perfect, crisp rectangular certificates with nails chewed down to the bleeding skin.

"Listen," Mommy said in a safe, practiced cadence, "Daddy will be home in a little while. Remember not to make too much noise. Did you want to move your books and things from the outside table now?"

Those were words of warning in my ears. Predicting Daddy's temperament was like predicting the future. At ten, I was not brave enough for that challenge. So I usually got my things off the outside table. There would be less chance of a meeting then.

I used to be afraid to talk when he came home because he studied a lot and said that good children played dead. If dogs could do that, then so could clean, bright children.

No noise, no trouble.

No trouble, no beatings.

Business as usual.

During my father's temperamental times, Mommy waited silently on the small plaid sofa opposite the table where my father would sit eating his supper. The sofa rested on carpet pieced together through the years from what the salesman called "remnants." About twenty-seven different pieces of carpet covered the living room, foyer and hallway outside my bedroom. Some were floral patterns, others geometric designs and the remaining were solid colors. The plaid sofa sagged on top of it all. Scary colors, lines, demented flowers, all mismatched and pieced together without order or size considered. Staring at it too long could cross your eyes. It was Carpet Crayola for the criminally inclined. Carpet Lego for the uncoordinated all put together by an interior decorator on a cheap budget and a questionable grasp of coordinating colors.

Mommy, her body delicate and still, her heart quickly palpating under her avocado colored shirt like those tiny birds on PBS, waited with her hands firmly folded in her lap. Her eyes fixed on my father's face. Her ears alert, ignoring the muffled banter of the evening news, readily locked on the frequency of her husband's voice. Any dinnertime request for condiments, juice, or extra napkins would not go unheard. If the king felt taken care of, if the dishes came and went with precision, then the peasants could be happy.

For Daddy, love was obedience. "My wife and daughter show their love through obedience. And a child's job is to be obedient. Always."

Sometimes Daddy said that I didn't love him. But that, I know for sure, wasn't true. It was just that I used to be afraid to talk in his presence. Keeping quiet would assure me that nothing stupid would be said on my part. That was one thing that could be predicted. If Daddy was around, then I would surely put both feet into my mouth. Now that could be predicted.

But usually, after he finished his meal and all his work was done for the night, he stopped by my room to laugh about something. All the time.

Daddy's laughter usually signaled a beacon that the next day or two would be good. All defenses would be off, and no one would have to play dead for a while.

Affection, like laughter, was earned. This did not make sense to a ten year old who somehow knew that love and affection could not be doled out on a token economy. It just wasn't normal. And it seemed really odd especially when my friends' families exchanged hugs and kisses so freely with me, and I held back. The one time I did initiate a hug with my friend, almost instinctively and out of the blue, it frightened me so much that I walked home in shame.

Those were usually the times I would think about my brother. Yes, if he were here I would hug him and not let go. He would be coddled and cleaned, and his little baby clothes would be ironed and ready by his crib. Milk would be warmed and waiting. I would help Mommy with everything. He wouldn't leave then. How could he leave with his clothes all ready and his milk all warm like that?

· ❖ ·

"Kamilya, it is bound to happen one day," my father said. "Watch and see. One day you'll get married, too. And then your last name will not be Khan anymore. You'll be Mrs. So and So. And maybe, maybe he'll be a doctor or a lawyer...or an accountant like your cousin Nageeb."

Yuck, was my first and final thought on the matter. First of all, one of the things that I did remember from Sunday School was that there was nothing in the Qur'an that said I had to change my last name. And anyway, why get married? So I could be the fetch and fix-it dog for some exceptionally unsociable, emotionally frozen boy. A boy pickled in his work-clothes or tickled by the sound of stock reports and monogrammed stationary. A carefully spoiled boy. The core rotted apple of some stately woman's eyes. The son of a doting mother with fat rosy cheeks whose bag always matched her shoes.

That was not going to be for me.

And if I wanted affection why would I want to be married to a boy like that?

Or would it be a marriage like my parents'? A marriage in which affection was like the fickle currency traded in the dark corners of a seemingly civilized world. A world in which moist green bills were shifted, folded and rubberbanded in knots, then secretly deposited from hand to hand; finally disappearing without notice.

"She didn't turn out the way I expected," was what Daddy said on his temperamental days. When he told the story, his eyes glared to the left as though the past were nailed, dry, dusty and hollow, like the scaly molted shell of an insect, to the corner of the apartment. My spine shook while watching his hand squeeze his wrist. The story was the same each time.

"So there I was in America with two kids and the sudden realization that she was not who I wanted her to be. I couldn't do anything about it because divorce is a shame in our community, and two kids need a stable home. What would people say back home? You were both so little. And then your brother became ill. It was too trying on your mother and I. Then, he passed away. What was I to do? Put another nail in his coffin? In your mother's heart? Your mother became sad. Completely unconsolable. It was too late. I couldn't leave her like that. It was just too late. I was responsible for giving you a good home. Having food on the table. A good, stable home."

A stable home? Where? Where is that stable home? There is no princess here. There is no castle with red and gold flags waving in the air. The king and queen have been dethroned, and the princess has been locked away in the dungeon. She asks not to be taken out. She is happy there and keeps company with her dreams. She wonders if the prince left before her because he knew what was to come.

· ❖ ·

My dreams give me fits. Sugrah says she understands. They are different from hers, but she says she knows. She says we feel the same. Zafran brings me aspirin and colorful vitamins wrapped in paper napkins, rubberbanded twice. Sometimes she brings me candy and Vicks. She says she'll help me just like she tries to help Sugrah.

"You two are the same," Zafran says. "Suck the candy and rub the Vicks on your forehead before you go to sleep. You'll feel better," she says while holding my hand during line up.

I do what she says, but it doesn't stop. I hit my face with the pillow, and I can't stop scratching my arms. I see myself jumping into a pit full of snakes and bugs and sitting in a bathtub full of dirty water and dead fish.

I see myself in some place full of thick story books, matching carpets and happy people. A perfect place where parents hug and kiss in front of their children.

Someone once told me that crying means you have given up. I cry all the time, but I have not given up. People disappoint me more and more, but I don't care.

I am in tenth grade now and nothing seems to surprise me anymore.

I'm still good, and I'm still hoping that I will love someone when I am older. I will be my love's garment, and he will be mine. We will be coverings for one another.

I'll be waiting with my goodness filled in all my pockets. Stuffed silky soft like a magician's unending trick scarf up my sleeve. My hands will be warm. My fingers will be whispering prayers at my side. My love will know me at once. I'll be the one with the halo of salt beneath my eyes. And when he touches my hand, he shouldn't worry if he doesn't feel a thing.

Matrimonials

❖❖❖

Ahmad ibn Hanbal chose a one-eyed woman rather than her sister,
even though the sister was beautiful.
He had asked which was the more intelligent of the two.
"The one with only one eye," they told him.
"Marry me to her," he said.
- Imam Al-Ghazali, "Adhab an-Nikah"

Family of Sunni Pakistani MBA residing in Los
Angeles, invite proposal for son, 27 yrs. 5'9".
Son seeks well-educated beautiful, fair skinned
girl, must be professional. Forward photo & bio
to Box 46663.

Egyptian Muslim, born in Alexandria, Ph.D. candidate
(biochemistry), has Green Card, 28 yrs. 5' 7",
seeks open-minded, well-educated Muslima from Egypt
or Arab country, bet. ages 18-24, nice looking,
that likes to be needed. Preferably a professional.
Must speak fluent Arabic. May be relocating to
Emirates. Box 23345.

USA born Pakistani Muslim physician, 32, divorced, fair, handsome, gentle, 6'1', seeking alliance from 19-26, good looking, never-married, slim Muslima of Pakistani or Indian background, MD., pre-med student or professional-type preferred. Chicago resident a plus. Box 45663 or E-mail: Zindabad@med1.org

Mother of handsome Sunni software engineer with Masters in computer science, 29, 5'10", 160 lbs, good looking, athletic, outgoing, seeks sophisticated, professional, slim and beautiful Muslima of Indo-Pak parentage. No divorced girls, please. Box 21334.

Ruby Auntie told me to keep my standards high and my motives true. She is my mother's youngest sister. Everyone thought she would never marry, so they were all shocked when she said yes to a Pakistani botanist six years ago. My family placed some matrimonial ads in two Muslim magazines, and the proposals came tumbling in. Photos, c.v.'s and E-mail from all corners of the world. I didn't know there were so many single Muslim men out there who wanted "slim, fair skinned *girls* under 30" from specific cultures. Girls? Funny, I thought I was a woman—or at least a young woman—and my culture is Islam.

Nan'na told Ruby Auntie that she shouldn't worry that she was not fair skinned. Her prospects were still good since she was still under 30. She was never married, had a Ph.D., was blessed with the advantage of height, had a good job, always wore conservative suits, and on top of it all, spoke fluent Urdu. Nan'na reminded Ruby that our family was well known in the community and that she had specified that only qualified young men need send their proposals.

After Na'na and Nan'na announced to the community that they were seeking proposals for their youngest daughter, Nan'na clamped her hand on the phone every time it rang. Her notebook and pen waited on the kitchen counter like a surgeon's tools. She picked up the phone with a thoroughly well rehearsed script in mind. Nan'na had it all figured out. Nan'na knew what she had to say and when to weed them out.

As she hung up the phone after speaking with an unlucky suitor, Nan'na said, "I may be old woman, but I can still tell decent man by sound of his voice." Nan'na suddenly became the Matrimonial Postmaster General. With phone in hand, she said that she could discern the First Class proposals from the flimsy Third Class proposals just by the way the men spoke about themselves. She had trained her ears to spot what she called the "deescrapancy" in the grainy undercurrent of a man's voice.

" I will know your future husband's voice. I will know it," Nan'na said to Ruby Auntie.

Ruby Auntie took a breath and held Nan'na's hand. "Not husband Ma, I don't want a 'husband'. I want a life companion."

"Oh husband, life companion, same thing. I raised such strange daughter. Same thing, both words mean same thing. Professor Ruby correcting her am'mi again."

"Ma, you know what I mean. Like a companion for the journey of this life and the next, Insha'allah."

"My daughter, she's good poet. Very inteleegent. Fine. Life companion. Well, first I have to hear his voice, then you can make decision. Your am'mi knows. I have ears trained for thees."

"I know that, Ma. Consider yourself fortunate. You are blessed in that arena."

Nan'na smiled mischievously and arched her eyebrows. She put her hands on Ruby Auntie and Mom's shoulders. "Your mother wants to protect daughters from weak men. You don't need weak man. I'm not afraid for investeegate. I'm not afraid for ask. If man's mother or father calls, I just tell them to put son on phone. What, I say, is son afraid to talk to me?. My daughter will not marry boy who can't speak by himself."

Then, with a pen firmly in her grip, she crossed out the name of a seemingly mute suitor from her perpetually changing list. "There," she said, "we don't have to deal with thees boy anymore. Maybe he will meet nice girl who only speaks through her parents, too, yes."

• ❖ •

Last month, after I graduated with my BA, I actually started to consider the idea of marriage. When I told Nan'na, she started getting out her jewelry and pulled out a red Samsonite suitcase full of shiny shalwar khameez. She said she wanted to be ready. After a week or so, my family's initial excitement was drowned out by my sudden change of heart. Nan'na wrapped all her jewelry in towels and put them back under her mattress. With the exception of a pink silk shalwar khameez that she hung on her closet door, the red suitcase, once again, took its place in the basement closet.

Nan'na pointed to the sophisticated pink suit embroidered with shimmering orange birds of Paradise. "It will be reminder," she told me. "A reminder that your Nan'na is ready when you are."

Then suddenly, two weeks ago, when I turned twenty-two, I told my parents I thought it was the right time for me to get married. I assured them that I was positive this time, that I had time to really consider it from all sides. It had clicked in my mind like a lost combination that was found by chance. I knew what I wanted. I knew what was in my heart.

So why wait. In the fall, I would be starting my Masters, so it wouldn't hurt to at least get the process started. It would be good to take a look at what kind of Muslim guys were out there. And if Ruby Auntie's life companion search was any indication, it would probably take a while.

Overjoyed at the decision, and simultaneously afraid that I would change my mind again, Mom immediately called Ruby Auntie and told her I was coming over.

"Talk some sense into her," Mom told Ruby Auntie. "And please, don't let her change her mind again. Ma even has her suit ready—again. She keeps on waving it in front of poor Amina like a racing flag when she passes her room to make wudu."

· ❖ ·

Ruby Auntie and I get along quite well. She is the complete opposite of my two other aunts, Nargeez and Saira. My mother's two elder sisters are too girlie, too old fashioned and too culture-drowned for me. I call them the Lahore Ladies of Stone because they refuse to wear foundation which matches the true color of their skin. They always yell at the woman at the Clinique counter when she suggests a slightly more natural shade of liquid make-up. They're nice enough, but a bit too unreasonable for me. I hate the fact that they tell me to take my hijab off. I mean, they should know that it's a Fard. Gee, I mean they were raised in Pakistan. I wasn't. You would think that they know more than me. But I guess they don't.

Nargeez and Saira Auntie are always squinting their noses at me. Telling me that I should be more like a lady. "You don't need to wear that horrible cloth on your head. You are still young, Amina. Go and perm your hair like Julia Roberts. With a little mehndi and some curlers, you'll look like twins. Take off those dirty jeans and put on a nice shalwar khameez or a nice dress. Something from Macy's, maybe. You know Macy's, right Amina? And stop replying to us in English." Their nasal diatribe pierced my eardrums, and I was immediately struck nauseous at the sight of their polished toenails choking under the tight criss-crosses of black leather straps.

The Greeks, I thought, had their chorus. I, on the other hand, had the Lahore Ladies of Stone in flowing georgette regalia and dangling, sheer dupattas. They complained to my parents every time they visited. They walked in, sat down, crossed their legs like gold medal synchronized swimmers, and then *it* began. With tea cups in their hands, they broke into the same routine each time.

Nargeez Auntie adjusted the dupatta on her shoulders and looked at my mother over the rim of a lipstick stained tea cup. "Can't Amina speak Urdu properly? How can you expect that girl to get a decent proposal if she doesn't even have the skills to speak to her future mother-in-law properly?"

Almost on cue, Saira Auntie joined in the critique as she fixed an unruly strand of hair behind her ear. "And those clothes, aren't those boy's jeans and shirts? A tomboy at her age. We must do something about that. Doesn't she have any friends who can show her how to dress?"

Ruby Auntie is different. She knows the deal. Ruby Auntie isn't into heavy make-up like Nargeez and Saira Auntie. That's why I think she's the prettiest one of my mother's sisters. Her real beauty shines through. She was the only one of my mother's sisters to have attended college in New York City. Although she doesn't always wear hijab, just like the rest of my aunts, she never tells me to take mine off. She always says that she appreciates how a young woman like me can have the strength to wear it. She looks at me through her cool eyeglasses and says, "You wear it well. I hope I'll have the courage to do it one day."

If Ruby Auntie doesn't like something about me, she tells me in a nice way. Not in a slow, fake voice, but completely straightforward and real. Ruby Auntie tells it like it is. She knows that I'm not a child anymore. She doesn't insult me or circle around the issue twenty times. She doesn't sugarcoat it or clam up when it's a sensitive thing. "Well, you know what I mean," is what she says. "You went to college, you know." That's why I knew that she would tell me how I was going to find Mr. Right—and what to look for in Mr. Right (or if he was even out there).

· ❖ ·

When I went to visit Ruby Auntie it was still a little early. She lives about ten blocks away, so I decided to ride my bike. Khalid, her husband, opened the door. He usually stays up after Fajr fiddling with his plants. He has about twenty in the front room. They're all set up in some kind of order. He has them in weird pots with thermometers and notecards sticking out. So you really have to be careful when you walk in. The last time I had gone over, I knocked down a tiny little plant with clover shaped purple flowers. Khalid didn't say anything, though. He wasn't mad or anything. He just kept mumbling something about starting over.

Ruby Auntie was in the kitchen grading some student papers. She was wearing oversized blue flannel pajamas with a big yellow smiley faced moon on the pocket. She was also wearing her favorite fuzzy house shoes.

When she saw me, she took her glasses off and stood up to hug me. "Oh, oh, Amina, oh my. The young *dulhan* of New York City! "

"Oh, really Ruby Auntie. How gross is that. No one is a *dulhan* yet. Please."

"Yes, the *dulhan* is here. Let me rephrase that, give me a moment. Um, um, okay, how about renegade *dulhan*?"

"Sounds better."

"Do you want some chai, coffee, some juice?"

"Yes, coffee sounds fine."

"Six teaspoons sugar, right?" Ruby Auntie asked with a smirk on her face. "What a sweet tooth you've got there. It will rot up your teeth before you hit thirty."

"No it won't. Nan'na told me that you and Mom have been drinking chai since you were little girls. And anyway Ruby Auntie," I said through a sharp smile, "it'll help me keep my eyes open through the lecture you and Mom planned."

Ruby Auntie nodded her head and looked at me over her frames. "Oh, so you were forewarned. Well, good then," she said as she gave me a little punch on my shoulders and then passed me a large mug of coffee and a canister of brown sugar.

"So tell me one thing," I said to her as I stirred in my fourth teaspoon of sugar. "What do you think about what Mom told you."

"Well, to tell you the truth," she said as she secretly counted my sixth and seventh teaspoons full of sugar , "I almost went into shock when your mother called last night. I was thinking it was yet another false alarm."

"No, I can assure you that I'm serious this time. I've had time to think it over. Clearly."

"Well, I can see that. I mean, Ma does have her famous pink suit ready."

"Nan'na is hilarious. She's nagging Mom about getting matching shoes. I keep on telling her that they don't make pink shoes anymore. She told me to look around for some anyway."

"Ma's funny like that. She's excited, you know."

"Yes, I love her. She understands. She was telling me about the whole voice thing. How she can tell if a guy is good or not by his voice."

"She is blessed. She has narrowed it down to a science. At least we can be glad that she is not peering at tea leaves. That would be embarrassing and considered *shirk*, I may add. So, how are you feeling about the whole idea of marriage?"

"Well, honestly, I'm just trying to get my expectations together."

"Anything specific in mind?"

"I guess I'll decide when the first proposals start to come in."

"You know, you just can't marry any Tariq, Jameel, or Har'ris that comes through the door."

"Of course. Come on Ruby Auntie, you know me."

"Yes, but you know, marriage is for life, Amina. You'll be living with the man, eating with the man, sleeping with the man, going on vacations with the man and whatever else. It's no joke. You have to know what you're looking for."

"I know. I think about that a lot. It's like a twenty-four hour companion, so you have to choose carefully."

"Yes, and more. It's more than that. You have to be selective and mature about the process. Just look at the family you come from. I know we aren't perfect—just look at your aunts. But at least everyone has some manners. We have a certain degree of education. It's not like we are all physicians and lawyers, but we try to be professional no matter what we do for a living. Look at your mother. She doesn't work; she didn't even finish college. But look at her, she has certain standards of adhab, of conversation and just plain interaction.

"You should think about these things. Think about what you want. We aren't like those women who forget that they have to grow as people—as Muslims—as well. You know the ones. The sisters who forget to mind their adhab in all aspects of life. The ones who talk through the entire Jumah khutba, the ones who crush you when you bend down to do sajdah, the ones who yell at you if you don't help them take care of their children, the ones who bully their way into leading taleem sessions—then gossip about everyone in the group. Do you want to be like them? What happens to those women? Where are their husbands? Have they forgotten to teach themselves and their families a little something about Islam. Aren't married people supposed to help guard one another's faith and taqwa? I suppose what I'm telling you is that you should consider choosing someone who can keep you growing. A covering for the soul, right? A person whose emotional and intellectual growth is not stunted after marriage. I'm sure you don't want to turn into a woman who *just* works, or *just* has kids, or *just* dotes on her husband."

"Well, no, of course not. I don't want to turn into *that* kind of person. I don't want to have that kind of marriage. No way. I mean, I'm looking for a man who can be my equal partner. A man who loves to tell me how he feels. Someone who will appreciate my poetry, my jokes—my attitude. A best friend, sort of. The type of person I can feel free with and say anything to. A man who is willing to be patient with my quirks and helps me to understand how I can be a better Muslim. A man who grows with me. I don't want a man to shove stuff down my throat. That's why I have Mom and Dad. Just kidding. I love them, you know that."

"Yes, I know. But you know, well, what you described. If you're really hoping for that, then in that case, you better not marry a guy from back home."

"You married someone from back home, right?"

"Yes."

"And your marriage is okay."

"Yes, it is."

"But?"

"But nothing. You, you're just special. You want

something real—and rare—and there's nothing wrong with that. But realistically, there aren't many men in this community who are like that. I mean what are we supposed to say to the families out here who have sons. That our Amina wants to marry a sensitive writer-type. I can see the look on people's faces when we tell them that. First of all, they probably wouldn't understand. They'll say, 'What writer, what is that. What kind of salary writer get? Tell her we have doctor for her. And engineer, too. Our nephew, he is engineer in California. Engineer is good income.' In addition, for them, anything that strays from their cultural views on marriage is a signal for rejection and gossip. They'll start spinning stories at their leisure. They're very creative when it comes to that. The phone-*fitna* club."

"I don't get that."

"Well try to because that's what we're dealing with. Remember Jen'nah?"

"Jen'nah Rahman?"

"Yes, well, Jen'nah married a very nice convert brother last year."

"Yes, I know him. Brother Hamza Sabur, he's really nice. He ran the Masjid day camp last summer when I was a counselor. Jen'nah invited me to the wedding but that was during finals, and I couldn't go."

"Yes, well, after the wedding people started spreading rumors about her saying that she had a relationship with him before she got married. That the marriage was forced by her mother to cover-up some bizarre goings on. It's a shame. You would think that they know that backbiting is equivalent to eating someone's flesh. It's as if a young woman can't marry someone outside the Indo-Pak community. Like there's something so strange about marrying a convert brother. They really need to wake up. Aren't we all converts? Weren't all new Muslims during the Prophet's* time converts as well?"

"Yes, but I think that's a little too logical for these people to understand. It's as though being born a Muslim actually determines one's true faith. How illogical is that. All the Sahaba were converts."

"You're completely right. That's a fact. But you forget, these people around here don't care about fact; they care about fiction. Fiction gives them an excuse to call one another."

"That's really pathetic. Sad. Do you think it will ever change?"

"Allahu Alim. You can't spend your life thinking about what people will say behind your back. If it's correct according to Qur'an and Sunnah, then there's nothing to be afraid of. And anyway, what you were saying, I think it's good. It's good that you've defined what you want. But remember, you can't always get what you want. You get what you can find. What's out there. And the last time I looked, there wasn't a giant crowd of single Muslim poets and writers out there."

"I'm not saying that the guy has to be quoting lines from Whitman and Sandburg. I just want someone who understands me. Who sees me in the way that Allah has made me: A person to be respected and loved. And, anyway, who says he has to be from back home. He just has to be Muslim. A real, practicing Muslim. Is that too much too ask?"

"No, it isn't too much to ask. And it is possible. It's actually quite noble. You just have to be willing to compromise. I doubt it's possible to have a custom-made companion. It's all about compromise, Amina. You know what your Nan'na says, 'all ten fingers are not equal.' "

"I think I've heard that saying a million times, and is that a line you older people use, 'compromise.' Is it in the How To Be A Cynical Adult Handbook?"

"No, but that's the reality, *beta*. You know, when I married Khalid it wasn't easy at first. But we made it work. I knew from the moment that I was first introduced to him that he was a genuinely nice man. Out of all the proposals, he was the first one who actually asked me what I liked, what I preferred in a companion. He actually used the word companion. It sounded poetic. He said 'humsaf'fer'. It was different. He didn't say husband. That gave it away for me that he was looking for a life companion and not a maid. There are enough maids in the world right now. He was a genuine find. A rare find. He even asked me about Islam in my daily life. He told me flatly, 'Love grows when you marry for the sake of Allah.' Who says *that* these days? You rarely find guys from back home who would even think of that. Mind you, I'm not trying to insult the guys from back home, either. And, anyway, he wasn't raised back home. He was raised here."

"But he was raised by Pakistani parents, right?"

"Yes, but somehow he managed to form a Muslim mind, not a Pakistani one. It doesn't matter where you are from. The question is: What are your opinions based on? He demonstrated to me at our first meeting that he had the ability to form opinions that were not solely based on culture. And he isn't, thank Allah, a typical Mother's Boy."

"You mean a Mama's Boy."

"Yes, that's what I mean. Anyway, don't use me as your example. Your situation is totally different Amina. You will find your life companion even if we have to search long and hard."

"Well, I don't care if it takes five years. I'm not going to settle for just some guy. I won't just settle for someone who is good enough. You know, there's got to be more than just good looks, a mega salary and an impressive degree. I mean, I know that a lot of young women love all that nice sounding stuff. It is nice, I suppose. And it shows that brothers and sisters are working hard out there. There's nothing wrong with it, but there has got to be something more."

"Like what?"

"Like spiritual love. Loving someone for the sake of Allah. Like something that can't be measured by worldly standards and expectations. Some element that goes beyond just pocket change and a nice house. Something beyond these stupid glittery weddings."

"What are you saying now, that you don't want a wedding?"

"No, I want a wedding. But I want a wedding that means something—a wedding in which I know all the guests. I mean, like in the past, I hated going to weddings. The bride just sits up front in a wicker chair with her head down. Her face is all painted like some bizarre Technicolor cartoon, and her hair is done up with like five bottles of hairspray—it's probably heavier than her whole body. Then all the ladies go up and lift her chin and then look at her face. That must be annoying. What's all that cultural stuff anyway? What? The bride has to appear pseudo-respectful or something? I didn't know that a lowered, depressed face passed as respect. That's all cultural. I know *that* isn't Islamic in origin. I'll probably be the first bride in the history of Pakistani weddings to actually look up, laugh, talk to my friends and actually move my head without help. I'll tell you one thing, I won't wear heels and I won't wear a hundred pound glittery dress. And please, tell Nargeez and Saira Auntie that lipstick and eyeliner are as far as I go."

"Are you from another planet, or are you just weird?"

"I guess I'm just different."

"But you know one thing?"

"What?"

"Different is good. Especially if you stick to what you expect and what makes you happy."

"What do you mean?"

"I mean that what you want is good. It's sincere and honest. It's what a true Muslim would want. It's unpretentious and real. What you expect is pretty fair. A little *too* specific, but fair nonetheless."

"Well, is there any other way?"

"Yes, but unfortunately that would be the way of culture."

"And culture is the rust of Islam—or is it nationalism?"

"Nationalism. Culture. Same thing. The only true criteria should be the strength of one's faith and character. Islam does not discriminate according to national or ethnic boundaries."

"I agree. Quite simply, marriage is a good thing. It's a part of the Sunnah. It's considered half the faith. Right, Miss Hadith?"

"Right. Absolutely. It is."

"Always be aware that you aren't the only one who thinks that way. There is a guy out there for you. He may not be in New York. He may not be on the entire East Coast."

"Thanks a lot. I mean, then where is he? Pluto?"

"No, I'm just teasing you. Look, he's out there. You're asking for a special type of a guy."

"I didn't know that a guy who likes books and nature, someone who respects women as prescribed by the Qur'an and Sunnah, a spiritual, sensitive guy was something too much too ask."

"And would you like him to have a BA in Literature and be exactly 5'7" just like yourself? Oh my, Amina. Please help me here, *beta*. You don't think it's too much too ask? Look at which community you're asking."

"Well, maybe he won't be from this community. Maybe he's living in some small Muslim community in the middle of the wilderness. Maybe he writes on bark paper, lives in a tent with a little fire burning outside, goes out to make wudu by a creek and then offers Salat with the wolves, prairie dogs and hedgehogs scurrying nearby. You're right. He's definitely out there. And maybe it will take five years because he has no parents, and he doesn't read those matrimonial ads in Muslim magazines."

"Alright, alright. You forgot the part about the adhan being called before a wispy twilight gloam. Wait. Wait a minute. I think I hear the violins in the background."

"Hey, c'mon now Ruby Auntie!"

"Don't worry. I get it. If he's out there, then we'll find him."

"Insha'allah. In the meantime, I'm keeping my expectations just like they are. Will you promise me one thing?"

"And what will that be?"

"Please try to explain all this to Mom and Dad and Nan'na. And one more thing."

"What?"

"Keep all the bios and c.v.'s of all those degree boys with no creative soul far away from me."

"I suppose I can manage that."

"Oh, I forgot, just one more thing."

"Yes, Master, what else?"

"A vegetarian."

"You're kidding, right?"

"No. I'm serious. He has to be a vegetarian."

"For that, we'll definitely have to go to Pluto—or comb all the vegetarian cafes from New York to Chicago, down to Santa Fe and all the way to Los Angeles for a sensitive, creative Muslim guy. I'll have to notify Khalid immediately. He'll need a good night's rest for that kind of search. We'll get our vegetarian sensors, sensitivity meters and writers' traps ready."

"The search is on then?"

"This is not just a search. This is a S.M.G.A."

"S.M.G.A?"

"Yes. Sensitive Muslim Guy Alert."

"Very funny."

"Well, you certainly aren't looking for the average guy."

"I suppose you're right. I suppose that's a good thing."

"It's what you want. That's all that is important. Keep the faith."

"Insha'allah."

Muslim-American, 28, Irish ancestry, teacher @ Muslim school, BA History & Education, writer, resides in mid-west, seeks dedicated Muslima 24-28 for life companionship. Background/culture not important, must be sincere, creative, nature enthusiast, must appreciate literature & be willing to accommodate a vegetarian, BA preferred (but not important). Box 21468.

The Charismatic

❖❖❖

"Some eloquence is like magic."
- Sahih Hadith

Eleven young women and five young men came to sit at Sister Maleeha's feet. She was going to teach them about Islam. She herself was the devoted student of a famous Sheikh. Maleeha had trekked to Europe, the Middle East, and California to sit by his knees and watch him expound on exegesis and utter fatwas from behind a smile as crisp as January rain. His eyes kept his students running from country to continent just so they could learn something—anything— as long as it was from a place close enough to wonder what his face looked like underneath his well-kept beard.

During scholarly retreats, his smiley faced, ether-scented acolytes, his adoring multicultural *taliboon*, flew in from all over the world. They nodded their heads in agreement as they watched him weave khutbas and lessons. He was simply the best, brightest and most compassionate. Through his popularity he had become the arbiter of etiquette and style. If he donned a navy thobe and a red kufi, then navy thobes and red kufis became the standard. If he gently kissed the

Qur'an before reciting a Surah, then they kissed the Qur'an harder. They did not hesitate. They did not question. For if the Sheikh did it, then it could never be an innovation—you only had to watch, and then follow.

Once in a while, there were those who questioned the Sheikh and asked for proof, some specific daleel or historical precedence from the Sunnah. This made the others who followed without question upset. The poor brother or sister who asked for clarification was persona non grata. If you made waves, your salams would not be answered, and you were encouraged—with a smiley face—that maybe the Sheikh's classes were a bit too intellectual for you to handle. *Go home. Take a little rest because obviously you're a little stressed, a little jealous of the Sheikh, perhaps, and maybe you'll be considered for admission next year. Okay brother? Remember, the Sheikh still loves you. Ma as-salam.*

On the last day of the retreat, the Sheikh's students would purchase lecture tapes, books and videos. They needed to spread his message. They wanted him close to their hearts. Others, they thought, should hear his beautiful words as well. What's better than to have a tape on hand to spread his words and philosophy to the naive masses who only relied upon the Qur'an and Sunnah exclusively.

When the Sheikh's students returned home, they watched his videos which—if only for a moment—replaced the longing they had for him in their hearts. On screen, his face, like a breathing moon, illuminated in a light so cosmic and clear, burst forth with such warmth and grace that they could do the one thing they had secretly wanted to do at the retreat: take the Sheikh's face in their hands and stroke it, like a trophy, like it was meant for them—and only *them*. How wonderful, they thought, to be so respected and have such admiration. And how marvelous—for them— to have been chosen to be in his company.

So as Sister Maleeha sat before her students and looked deep into their eyes, she knew they, like her, craved more than just a bit of tafseer or fiqh. They needed an identity built on association. For the power of name dropping added scholarship to one's presence. It did not matter if one was not well versed in Islamic knowledge. If one attended the Madrassa of the Stars you needed only one reference, one explanation for your actions: *I learned it from my Sheikh,* was all that needed to be said. It did not matter if you didn't wake up for Fajr, lied to your brothers and sisters in the name of some mythical justice, ate a Happy Mac Burger on your way home from college or work (The train was a hardship, right? And, anyway, one really needed some nutrition); or announced a *Sahih* hadith as *Dhaif* in the presence of the truth.

If a brother or sister dared to disagree with the basis of the Sheikh's decree after cross referencing his ideas with Qur'anic ayahs and Hadith, his loyal students would slowly attack the validity of the authentic proofs. Even if the Qur'an was opened in front of them, the exact Surah and ayah pointed to, they would not budge. Their blind trust of the Sheikh's words created an impermeable fortress that also worked to bolt shut the doors of logic in their mind. With this, the Sheikh was free to pick and choose the authentic proofs that supported *his* views.

Those few brothers and sisters who disagreed with his ideology were ignored and their proofs—as the students were taught to do with the precision of spear fishermen—pronounced sick or invalid. The devoted *taliboon* lived by one main rule: If an ayah or example from the Sunnah contradicted their Sheikh's ruling, then it should be thrown out.

The Qur'an and Sunnah were there, of course, if one cared to look, but Sister Maleeha's students, like Sister Maleeha herself, needed something more. *They needed a superstar.* For a superstar made Islam magical. Through a superstar, one could always get a reference and a mind-numbing performance. Why read the Qur'an yourself when you could have it interpreted for you, told to you, in a voice so sweet that the verses themselves became Top Forty Hits in your heart.

As the eleven young women and five young men looked at Sister Maleeha with the fixed gaze of fans, she knew that she had something special. They were young, empowered by the zeal to learn and blinded by naiveté. Their brains yearned for knowledge, and the dark void created by the lack of self-esteem made them yearn for easy, portable power.

Sister Maleeha had been their teacher for three years. They had been hers since they attended high school. Now, they were young college starlings growing underneath the sweetly oiled, vise-like grip of her tongue. She looked at their faces and saw the blush of her successful manipulation; the wide-eyed stare of a cultivated, necessary dependence. They needed her, just as *she* needed them. She was their smiling and lovable teacher. Their supple-faced mother superior who held a ruler behind her back. At times, she was firm and then after a moment, softened up after she had put them in their place. She humiliated them, broke them down emotionally, and then turned around with a smile on her face that made them feel like they could conquer the world with the little information they had. They were her students for life, and she was their superstar.

"Come to me," she said in her best lipstick voice (tuned to a British disciplinarian's cadence) to her college-aged fans. "Come to me beta, beti, and sit by your mother's feet. Shhh. Shhh. No questions. Not now. Later."

Then, after selecting a favorite student and telling the eager young woman to sit right by her side, she would open to the selected topic or the hadith of the day, and tell her to recite. "Yes, read this here, beti. Softly. Don't hurry. Did you not learn how to read in college? Were you born to illiterates? No, not like that. That's all wrong. Like this. Do you hear me? Yes, better. Very good. Now go back to your seat."

For the students who sat in her presence, Sister Maleeha wasn't insulting anyone. How could she be condescending when she was only trying to help, and with all that she had given them, they should be utterly grateful.

· ❖ ·

It could be said that all of us are looking for a little recognition; something to tide us over until we find ourselves worthy in our own eyes. Find that lost bone of self-worth, that magical cord of self-confidence that connects us to our healthy selves. In the meantime, if others are willing to give us the credit and adulation that we believe we so richly deserve, then what could be the problem? And if, perchance, we never find our healthy selves, then at least we have the lush carpet of praise to soften the fall—if, in fact, it ever comes.

One evening, after cutting morning classes to see a newly released Rekha movie at Pavilion Cinema, as she stepped out from a taxi at the gates of her parents' flat in Bandra, Maleeha knew that she wanted out. It was 1973, and she was twenty-two going on restless. After two years of studying Urdu Classics at Bombay University, she was nauseated by the young women who upstaged her by studying harder and having more knowledge about Urdu literary conventions than herself.

When she had first started attending the University, her professors always asked that she sit in the first row. Since she had the most melodic voice in the class, she was usually called on to recite the poem or short story which was to be analyzed for that session. However, after what occurred during this afternoon's class, she never wanted to see another University class again.

It began in a rather harmless way. As usual, she was selected by the professor to recite a poem. Today's poem was a rather lengthy spiritual meditation on the intrinsic worth of love by the poet Iqbal. After recitation, when she was asked for her interpretation, Maleeha's mind came to a blank. Her strength, after all, was in the art of voice, not in literary analysis. She had been asked before for such analysis, but usually smiled and said that she was so overtaken by the poem's emotion to respond critically.

But today, she was caught off guard because her mind was with Rekha and Amitab Bachan frolicking in the rain on some majestic Kashmiri hillside. When put on the spot, she thought of something to say—quickly. And why not? She was one of the prettiest girls in class, and everyone was very jealous of her voice. So what if she didn't understand the poem. She would say what came to her mind. Maleeha looked at her classmates, swung her hair over to one side, and cleared her throat. "Well, how romantic. Ahem, ahem. The poem is quite good, really. It is so.....sweet. Very soft and lovely, but a bit too long, no?"

The class stared at Maleeha in shock. The room was silent. The professor coughed, wiped a handkerchief over his forehead, and rolled his eyes. Then, from the third row of the lecture hall, a young woman wearing thick glasses in square black frames, whose shalwar khameez was obviously a hand-me-down, started to laugh. Softly at first, and then, as though she could not hold it in any longer, burst forth to reverberate the room in snorting guffaws. This cleared a boulder from the entire class' throat. In no time, buckets of laughter and strident echoes of mimicry *"a bit too long, no?"* began to fall around the room, swift and relentless like a monsoon rain.

Maleeha's nostrils flared like gills and the skin on her face turned red and bumpy like the center of a pomegranate. She grabbed the microphone in her hand and yelled as hard as she could, "You bloody fools! How dare you! I am Maleeha! I am Maleeha Maimoon! I will be somebody one day, and you will all be stuck sweeping the gutters of Bombay!" Then she grabbed her bag from the center of the first row and ran out of the room with her lime green lace dupatta dragging behind her like a limp, broken tail.

· ❖ ·

Mr. and Mrs. Maimoon did not make an issue out of their daughter's decision to leave the University. She would be married in a year, and with her good looks, fair skin and fine family background, a degree did not matter in the least. However, if she were a bit darker and not that attractive, then a degree would boost her prospects. But their Maleeha, the beautiful fruit of their love, had been receiving proposals for the last three years. They were ready to have her married, but Maleeha told them she wanted to be a poet, and that she wanted to study at the University. Well, with her lovely voice, their daughter would make a marvelous poet. But that was before this incident. Before she was humiliated by jealous classmates who wished in their dreams that they could be as lovely as Maleeha. Well, they could never be because, of course, there could only be one Maleeha: Mr. and Mrs. Maimoon's doll-faced daughter.

After releasing herself from the constraints of her academic life, Maleeha found herself with hours and hours of free time. She visited the Pavilion Cinema, shopped in the afternoons at Benzer's and Amarson's, and browsed for hours at Sweet Melody House purchasing an armload of records at each visit. After dinner, she sat on her bed and wrote down the lyrics of her favorite songs. The next day, after committing the songs to memory, she performed them in front of her parents on the living room balcony. Her parents were so proud of her voice, that her father ordered a professional microphone from a bank associate in Hong Kong. Now his daughter could sing like a true chanteuse.

Maleeha practiced the songs in her room. She learned to hold the microphone with style, like she had seen the singers do in the movies. She held the microphone like a cigarette, slowly bringing it to her mouth as she swayed side to side, swishing her hair in synchrony with the rhythm.

Mrs. Maimoon admired her daughter's talent and believed that if she took it seriously, then there was a chance. Just as Maleeha had won third place in the Young Poets Contest, she had the potential to succeed with singing as well.

As Maleeha practiced her songs one evening, Mrs. Maimoon knocked on her door. She walked in and kissed her daughter. Then, as she took Maleeha's hand and looked into her eyes, she started to speak in her softest voice. "Dream big Maleeha. If you dream big, then even if you get a small piece of your dream, you will feel happy. And don't worry. Your father and I are dreaming for you, too."

After the talk, Mrs. Maimoon took her daughter by the hand and showed her the surprise that awaited her on the dining room table. A white box, large enough to fit Maleeha herself, sat underneath a mound of red satin bows.

"Go ahead," Mrs. Maimoon said, "go ahead, Maleeha. It's a gift just for you."

Maleeha was overjoyed. In her eagerness to open the box, she did not realize that she still had the microphone in her hand. As she tried to open the bow, the cord became entangled. After a few moments of frustration, she looked at what was in her hand. She laughed at her mistake, put down the microphone and eagerly got back to the business of opening her very large gift box. With the bows off, she carefully lifted the lid and gasped. Right there in front of her were six beautiful custom-made dresses. Dresses that were exact copies of the ones that her favorite actresses wore in the movies. Dresses that symbolized the songs Maleeha had memorized.

Maleeha pulled a yellow silk dress out of the box and held it under her chin. "Oh Mother, it's beautiful...they're all beautiful."

Mrs. Maimoon looked at her daughter and smiled. "Well, Maleeha, you will need them for your performances."

Maleeha's eyes screamed with glee as she threw her hands up in the air in disbelief. "My performances?"

"Yes. Your father asked his friend, Mr. Adnan Chand, at the Oberoi Hotel on Marine Drive, if you could have a chance to sing while their contracted singer goes on holiday. He sweetly asked if 'My Maleeha could have a go.' Mr. Chand said it would be a pleasure. After all, your father did approve his loan last month."

Maleeha couldn't believe her luck. If only her classmates could see her now. Who would be laughing at her now? No one. She was Maleeha Maimoon, and her name—

not theirs—would be glowing on the marquis at the famous
Oberoi Hotel.

· ❖ ·

They were from Europe, America, the Middle East and from
right there in Bombay. They came from Bandra, Carter Road
and Marine Drive. Only the finest. You couldn't get a room
at the Oberoi if you were a nobody. And you couldn't afford
to have reservations for dinner at the Oberoi's dining hall,
the Marine Grill & Lounge, if you were on a budget.

Maleeha asked her chambermaid to get her a dish of
masala shrimp and tea with honey (for her voice). Mr. Chand
was so nice. He always made sure she had everything she
needed. "The audience, they love you," he said to her after
every performance. And they truly did. She was enchanted.
She loved the clapping and the chorus of "bravos." Most of
all, she loved the flowers and gifts that suitors sent to her
dressing room at the end of each performance. One in
particular, a certain Dr. Jameel Risvi, had sent her floral
arrangements, as large as her dressing table, each and every
night since she started performing two weeks ago.

Tonight, when the chambermaid returned with a tray
of shrimp and steaming hot tea, there was a small blue envelope
on top of an almond pastry.

"I did not order a pastry," Maleeha said to the chambermaid.

The chambermaid nodded her head and put the tray on a table full of colorful vases filled with large, tropical flowers. "Yes, Madam. I apologize. But a gentleman requested that you accept it on his behalf. I can take it back if Madam wishes."

Maleeha picked up the envelope and put it in her pocket. "No, that won't be necessary. But I would like my dress to be pressed, immediately."

"Yes, Madam, of course."

With the chambermaid gone, Maleeha put her feet up on the teak tipoy and slid her index finger under the flap of the letter.

```
Dear Miss Maleeha,
Please excuse my abruptness.  I have made up
my mind.  I have asked your father for your
hand in marriage. He has said it is your
decision. I will be in the audience tonight.
                 Sincerely,
                 Dr. Jameel Risvi
```

Well, who does this character think he is, Maleeha thought. *He has spoken to my father already. What gaul! I don't even know him.* As she carefully folded the letter back in the envelope, she smiled. *Well, he is brave. And he knows what he wants. The least I could do is call Father, so we could meet with him tonight. He isn't some roadside Romeo. He is a doctor. And if he's staying at the Oberoi, he does have some class. What could be the harm? It just might be a fun excursion.*

The chambermaid returned and announced that the curtain would go up in five minutes. "Listen," Maleeha told her as she handed her a business card, "dial this number and ask for Mr. Maimoon. Tell him that Maleeha wants him to come to the show this evening to meet Dr. Risvi."

· ❖ ·

Dr. Jameel Risvi was, indeed, a medical doctor. As he dipped a bhajya into some mint chutney, he told Maleeha and Mr. Maimoon that he had big dreams. He wanted to move to America. He would establish a practice in New York.

Maleeha liked a man with big dreams—and a man who was smart. A man who told her that *she* was smart, too. Jameel told her that he would take care of her in the style that she was accustomed to—this pleased Mr. Maimoon. It would be an adventure to move to New York, he told Maleeha. And in New York, Maleeha would personally see what she had only glimpsed before on TV.

"Just like that show, Daddy," Maleeha said while tugging at her father's sleeve. "Like that show on the television

that comes from America. I think it's called *That Girl*."
Maleeha's mind floated on the vision of an independent,
smartly dressed American Girl throwing her hat in the wind
that swept between the skyscrapers of Manhattan. I will also
throw my hat up in the air, thought Maleeha. I will be that
girl.

She is a forward thinker, Jameel thought to himself.
He wanted a forward thinking wife. A wife who was ready to
see beyond what was in front of her. She was a visionary, he
told her. He wanted to be somebody just like her, but staying
in Bombay was stunting. That's why he wanted them to shift
to New York after their Ni'kah. "Why not?" Maleeha agreed,
"Let's go."

In New York, their money did not go as far as it did in
Bombay. Maleeha and Jameel had to settle for a one bedroom
apartment in Kew Gardens, Queens—instead of an apartment
overlooking the East River in Manhattan (which was what
Maleeha had originally wanted).

Everything was so difficult. Jameel found out that
his medical license was just a piece of paper in New York. If
he wanted to work as a doctor, he would have to take a host
of courses from an accredited medical college and then take
an American licensing exam. That would all cost money.
Lots of money. Money they didn't have because he refused
to allow Maleeha to sing in New York. Back home it was one
thing, but here, in New York, a woman singing in a club or

restaurant was like prostitution. It was, as he began to justify, also *un-Islamic*. Yes, he had done a lot of things that were un-Islamic back home, but now that he was in America, things would be different. Here, in a city where the unacceptable was executed, accepted and advertised shamelessly on every corner, Islam suddenly gained back its appeal.

Jameel and Maleeha found a Masjid close to their home. There, they met other couples and families who were trying to adjust to life in New York. It was a struggle for some of them as well. The professional men, the doctors and engineers, told Jameel that it would take a while to get his medical license. In the meantime, how about driving a taxi, they suggested.

Jameel already had a driver's license, and one of the brothers at the Masjid who drove a taxi part-time, leased it to Jameel forty-five hours a week for a reasonable fee. It was hard work, but the money was steady. Maleeha didn't approve. She said she didn't want to be married to a taxi driver. Jameel explained to her that it was just temporary, but she would not listen. He told her that she need not worry. They were not in dire straits as long as he worked. And in time, he would save enough money to take the few classes that were required before he took his licensing exam.

Maleeha became frustrated with Jameel's long hours and soon grew tired of endless afternoons spent browsing through Queens Center Mall. She found herself spending more and more time at the Masjid. One day, after Jumah prayer, she met a very friendly sister. She, like Maleeha, was also from Bombay. In fact, her family lived at the Malabar Vista Flats right there in Bandra near her parents. Maleeha thought the sister was very intelligent, very classy. She asked Maleeha if she had heard of the Sheikh. Maleeha said she hadn't seen any of his lectures, but she had heard of him.

The sister asked Maleeha if she was free to attend a lecture on Saturday night. "It would be worth your while," the friendly sister said. "The Sheikh inspired me to come back to Islam. I was lost back home in Bombay. I thought Islam was just bothersome. No one really practiced it. We went to the Masjid on Eid, and Mum'i gave me a taveez to wear around my neck for good luck. I did a lot of wrong things, but the Sheikh let me know that I could always come back to Islam. And if I put my trust in him, then he would show me the way back. And he has."

Maleeha went to the lecture and realized that she, too, had found her way back. She had never studied the Qur'an or Sunnah on a scholarly level, but what the Sheikh said sounded good. He had such a wonderful voice. At the end of the lecture, the friendly sister introduced Maleeha to the Sheikh. He invited her and Jameel to an intensive seminar at the end of the month. Jameel would be working, but Maleeha was free. She said she was honored. She would attend.

"Sister, you can read the Qur'an in Arabic, can't you?" asked the Sheikh.

"Why, yes. Of course," said Maleeha while adjusting her hijab. "Most Muslim parents in India try to make sure that their children can *at least* read the Arabic text."

"Well, then, we would be blessed if you would agree to be one of our recitors, " the Sheikh said. "You would not have to give a commentary because I do that. You would just have to read, Insha'allah."

The friendly sister stroked Maleeha's shoulder and turned to the Sheikh, "Sister Maleeha has a beautiful voice, Ma'sha'allah. Don't you agree."

The Sheikh agreed. Maleeha did have a wonderful voice, indeed.

• ❖ •

After the first retreat, Maleeha was pleased. She had finally found herself a niche where she was recognized and appreciated. Her recitation at the first retreat proved to her that she still had it. Not only were people willing to listen, so many complimented her voice. "You are blessed with the voice of an angel," they said with smiles that reminded her of her fans at the Oberoi almost a decade ago.

Under the Sheikh's watchful gaze, after having attended quarterly retreats and intensive seminars in Chicago,

Los Angeles, London, and Amman, Maleeha emerged as a rising star. The Sheikh advised her to start her own youth classes in Kew Gardens. "Feel free to use me as a reference," he said. He asked his secretary to arrange the rental of a small office space that could be used as a classroom. As long as Maleeha agreed to pay for half the rent, the space would be hers.

Student tuition would not yet fully cover her half, so Maleeha asked Jameel. He was more than happy to do anything that would keep Maleeha from trotting around the world for the sake of her beloved seminars with the Sheikh. He had never questioned her desire to learn about Islam, and he always permitted her to do whatever made her happy. Yes, it was a strain on their marriage, and he really could not afford the airfare and other "necessary expenses" for comfortable traveling. But he did not want to discourage her. He did not want her to fault him.

As time passed, he realized that it would be a long time before he would be financially capable of going back to school. So, in the meantime, he could try his best to keep Maleeha content in *her* interests. Jameel's support of Maleeha's excursions and classes helped eliminate Maleeha's daily lamentation of "I cannot believe I married a bloody taxi driver." Jameel no longer felt like he was a shame to his wife. As long as he supported her, she left him alone. One thing that she did warn him about was never to get in her way. She was going to make it with *or* without him. So if he wanted to be by her side, if he wanted to have the benefits that being *Mr. Maleeha* could bring, he should not muddle in her affairs. *She controlled her schedule, not him.* If she couldn't make a name for herself in music, if she couldn't be a doctor's wife, then she would make a name for herself as a teacher of Muslims. Everyone would slowly get to know *Sister* Maleeha Maimoon.

· ❖ ·

The classroom was small, but it would do. There was a water cooler in the corner and two ferns propped up on a particle board table in front of the window. The carpet was a dull gray and very worn. It would do. Sheets were spread on the floor for her students, and a small, upholstered settee, that one of Jameel's customers had forgotten in the taxi's trunk, was placed at the front for Maleeha.

There were only two or three students at first. The daughters of some friends at the Masjid. Fresh faced high school girls whose parents recently immigrated from Pakistan and India. They listened to Maleeha with great interest. She knew things they did not. She had been to places that they had only seen photographs of in an encyclopedia. Maleeha was nicer than their parents, at first. She sat with them after class and even brought them some french fries or ice cream on certain days. Could they call her during the week if they had a problem, they asked. "Of course," she said. "From now on, think of me as your teacher *and* best friend."

The girls told their friends about Maleeha and slowly the class increased from three girls on Saturday and Sunday, to ten, eleven students every other day. Some were recent converts. Others were born as Muslims and were returning to Islam after living with parents whose ideas about Islam were purely cultural in origin. These youngmen and women had Muslim names, but after years of only practicing Islam on Eid, they had no clue what she was talking about. Although they did not understand everything she spoke about, they were confident of one thing: Maleeha was the friendliest and most cultured person they had ever met.

They lingered for hours after class, talking about their lives, mistakes, loves and dreams. Maleeha listened to each one with the attention of a private counselor. She nodded her head at the right time; stroked shoulders and held hands when the girl or boy started to cry as they told stories about demanding mothers, physically abusive fathers and classmates who teased them about their love for Islam. Girls who did not wear hijab previously, wanted to wear ones just like Maleeha's after attending the meetings. Boys who once cursed like truck drivers began to sprinkle phrases like Insha'allah, Ma'sha'allah, and Alhamdolillah liberally in their speech.

They still had a lot to learn Islamically, such as how to offer Salat properly, the fundamental sources of Islamic knowledge, and the criteria for sound Hadith. However, Maleeha instinctually knew that she had to cover topics that young people would be interested in first—if not, they would become bored and leave. So she discussed the Islamic merits of love and marriage, described the Gardens of Paradise in great detail, and talked about the Prophet's* relationships with his wives and children. It was all presented with enthusiastic flavor. The students were giddy with questions: "Tell us about the Prophet's* features—was he a handsome man?"; "What kinds of wishes can we make in Paradise?"; Is it okay to talk to a boy on the phone?"; "If I wear a jilbab, do I get into Paradise quicker than those who wear dresses and American clothes?"

After a year of being under Maleeha's tutelage, the young women became miniature Maleeha's and the boys wanted to marry someone "just like Sister Maleeha." They frequented her apartment after class for snacks and watched the Sheikh's videos together. The Sheikh, they agreed, "was very cool." Maleeha continued attending the Sheikh's seminars and instructed her students with bits and pieces of what she was taught.

When the students started to attend various colleges, they asked Maleeha to lecture at their MSA functions. Jameel happily drove Maleeha all around the city so she could lecture, run workshops and teach young Muslims. The young men shook his hand and told him he was so lucky to be married to "such a great Sister."

As Maleeha's influence increased, she decided that she no longer had to answer questions at the end of her lectures. She felt personally slighted and insulted by requests for specific daleel. If a few young people raised their hands to ask questions, one of her own students would whisper something in their ears and cause them to take a seat.

Maleeha's lectures were filled with emotion. She oftentimes started to cry in the middle of a story as she recounted her life as a "sinful singer" in front of her audience. "I used to sing for customers," she cried, "but now, I sing for Allah." She told the story of her mother, who died without ever fasting a single day in her life and of her father who utilized and encouraged riba his entire life. Her hands articulated suffering, warmth, hope, forgiveness—and finally redemption.

When she finished her lecture, the audience yelled "Takbir." As she walked back to her seat on the dais, she was hugged by a throng of young women and girls who flooded the stage; each one fighting to touch Sister Maleeha; each one calling themselves her daughter—except one.

· ❖ ·

At the refreshment table outside the lecture hall, Jasmine looked at her friend Kamilya over a plate of samosas. "Wasn't she great. I told you, it was going to be worth your while."

Kamilya was distracted. A small, noisy crowd of MSA sisters had gathered a few feet away. They circled around Sister Maleeha like helpless baby chicks, hands fluttering and mouths open waiting for their mother to regurgitate the day's treats into their mouths.

"I'm sorry. What did you say Jasmine?"

"I *said*, wasn't she great."

"Well, she seems nice, but why does she talk with that fake accent?"

Jasmine rolled her eyes. Offended that her friend could make such a remark about her wonderful teacher. "It's not fake. It's her style. Anyway, did you like her lecture?"

"Yeah, it was alright. I suppose. I have a few questions, though."

"Like what? I mean, she did explain everything."

"Well, for example, why is every other thing she says a from that Sheikh that she keeps on mentioning? I mean, aren't we supposed to consult with authentic sources, like Qur'an and Hadith, first."

"Yes, I suppose. But she doesn't mean any harm. And anyway, nothing she said was that bad. Just look at the way she spoke. She is so kind."

"I don't know. I just think that if you're going to be speaking in front of a group of college students, that the least you could do is provide some references so that I can go home and do the research on my own if I have any questions."

"Look, that's not a problem. Like I said, I'm sure she has references. She probably didn't want to drone on with technicalities and all that. Hey, look, she's right there. Why don't you ask her yourself?"

Jasmine took Kamilya by the elbow and walked over to Sister Maleeha who was slowly eating from a dish of mixed fruits that one of her students held in her hand.

"Sister Maleeha, Assalamu Alaikum," said Jasmine.

Maleeha, quickly swallowing a piece of fruit, turned around. "Oh, my Jasmine! My favorite student! Wa Alaikum as-Salam."

Jasmine tugged Kamilya by the sleeve and pulled her towards Maleeha. "Sister Maleeha, this is my friend Kamilya."

Maleeha reached our her hands and cupped Kamilya's hand warmly and snugly in hers. "Assalamu Alaikum, my daughter. My dear, are you a student here?"

"Yes, I am."

"Well, what are you studying?"

"Cultural Anthropology."

"Oh, how nice," Maleeha said as she slowly stroked her chin. "You're going to be a scholar, then."

Kamilya, eager to ask her question, curtly answered. "I don't know, yet. I still have two more years."

Maleeha looked at Jasmine with inquisitive eyes. "Jasmine, where have you been hiding your friend. You should bring her to my class."

"Oh yeah, I was going to ask her," said Jasmine as her hands fumbled in the air nervously as though she were trying to restrain a slippery fish in her grip. "I mean, I had it on my mind. But um, um, she had a question. Right, Kamilya, you had a question, right?"

"Sister Maleeha, I was wondering. Um, you said in your lecture..."

Before Kamilya could ask her question, Maleeha looked her with piercing eyes and nodded her head. "Beta, this is not a place to have an argument. We should behave like sisters. It is not proper adhab to try to contradict your elder sister."

Kamilya was puzzled. "Please, excuse me. I think you misunderstood. I'm not trying to contradict you. I just had a question—from your lecture. You said that it was better to marry from your own culture; that it's a primary indicator of a marriage's success. But according to Qur'an and Hadith that's not correct. In fact, the Prophet* said that the best reason to marry someone is on the strength of their faith, their taqwa."

Maleeha pursed her lips and asked Jasmine to get her a glass of water. Her voice no longer rode the smooth melody of confidence. Instead, it suddenly cracked and took shelter in the shroud of a disciplinarian's cape. "Beta, I'm not here to argue," said Maleeha. "There's no need to insult me. What is the problem, really? I think that this is not a valid question. You have a problem with me. Beta, why don't you relax and just tell me what is really bothering you?"

Kamilya, perplexed by her response, arched her eyebrows and looked at Maleeha straight in her eyes. "Excuse me, Sister Maleeha, I don't have a problem with anyone. I'm just asking you a question. If you are just espousing your opinion, then clarify. And if there is proper daleel for your statements, then help me to understand them."

"Listen *beta*, apparently you have some personal problem with me," said Maleeha as she issued a few strident laughs to hide the anger that slowly started to seep into her eyes like a blood-red fog. "You know, a good Muslim respects her elders. You cannot just come in front of me and try to insult me like that. You can't contradict me in front of others. Are you trying to divide the Ummah? You know that's a sin. You are dipping your foot in sin my dear child."

Kamilya took a deep breath and relaxed her arms by her side. "Sister Maleeha, I don't think you're understanding what I asked. I'm asking you a question. A question. I have a question. I'm not blaming you for anything, and I'm not trying to divide anyone. All I would like to know is what is the daleel for your statement?"

By this time, a small crowd of young women had gathered around Maleeha. Kamilya stood alone on the opposite side of the group.

Some of women who stood behind Maleeha started to mutter. "Look," one of the young women shouted at Kamilya, "don't bother our teacher. Take your personal issues elsewhere."

"I don't have personal issues," Kamilya said with quiet firmness. "I only have *a question*. But apparently, your teacher does not take *questions*. Anyway, excuse me sisters for bothering your teacher. Allah knows best. Assalamu Alaikum."

Kamilya realized that she could not have a discussion with someone who refused to provide evidence from Qur'an and Sunnah. It was like arguing with the deaf, dumb and blind. As she quietly turned around to leave, she heard the group of women laughing behind her.

Maleeha emerged from their midst and called out to Kamilya who was walking slowly towards the exit stairwell. "You see," she said to the young women as she raised her hand to point at Kamilya, "the *Shaitan* always runs from the truth."

A Doctor In The Family

❖❖❖

"A person will die with many sins and he will wake up without sins
on the Day of Judgment.
He will ask Allah (swt) with great surprise about his sins,
and Allah (swt) will answer him,
'You left good children behind who prayed for you and that's how
We have washed your sins.' "
- Tirmidhi

*I will be a doctor. A physician. A Board Certified Medical Doctor.
I will wear a white coat, and my chest pocket will be filled with a
Mont Blanc pen and a pair of expensive, yet utilitarian, glasses.
My parents will be proud of me. My friends will look at me in
awe. It doesn't matter if I have to take loans out from the bank,
because my intention is to help the sick and that is what ultimately
counts. I will be part of a noble profession. I will become a role
model. My parents will proudly say, "Our son is a doctor." That
sounds nice, doesn't it?*

Every night since he received his MCAT scores, Iqbal
Ahmed's dream was the same. He found himself walking in
narrow hospital corridor illuminated by fluorescent tube

lighting. It smelled like antiseptic. Clean and sharp like someone had sopped down the walls with iodine, alcohol and bleach. He followed the lights which stretched like neon tracks through an endless tunnel and headed toward an open door of an even more brightly lit office.

Iqbal put his hand through the open door and immediately felt cold. It was a doctor's office, or so it seemed because of the MD diploma and medical school certificates and honors hanging on the wall. But it was much too large to be just an office.

On the right side, there was a huge window, almost the size of the entire wall. All Iqbal could see was a clear blue sky just like they have in cartoons.

On the left, there were two bookshelves crowded with JAMA journals, manuals, medical models and complimentary pharmaceutical sticky notes. The bookshelves met at a perfect right angle of well polished oak. The office was clean, impressive and impeccably furnished.

In the center of the room there was a huge desk, like the kind you see a judge sitting behind on Court TV. There was a brass nameplate on the desk which glistened like a rectangular jewel. Iqbal squinted his eyes to read the name. He could not make it out. The name was indecipherable because of the complicated inscription which was in some kind of squirly, formal script.

A well-built man, about six foot five with graying temples, suddenly appeared behind the desk. He coughed twice and then threw his feet up on a mammoth mahogany desk. He was a well dressed gentleman. He wore a classy gray suit and a blue shirt. The collars were pinned in place with a silver bar attached to a little chain securing a red and gold striped tie.

Iqbal looked at the man closely. He noticed a strange family resemblance. The man could have been his uncle, his father even.

The man stared at Iqbal for a long time before speaking. It was a friendly stare, full of caution and consideration, so the young man did not worry. It was about then that the man started to laugh. It was a disciplined roar more than a simmer of chuckles. A well practiced torrent of chortles, rather than a simple, short, reserved "Ha, ha."

Frightened by the laughs, Iqbal quickly turned to leave, but the man called him back. He told him to sit down on the leather chair in front of the desk.

"Iqbal, sit down. Relax. Tell me a little about yourself. Like, for example, what score did you earn on the MCAT's?" the man asked while running his hands through his salt and pepper hair.

Iqbal folded his hands in his lap. He was proud of his score, but he did not want to brag. So he just said that the score was good enough to get into a blue chip medical school.

"How nice for you young man," the man said while flipping a silver pen in between his thumb and forefinger like whirling helicopter blades. "But tell me one thing: Who do you really want to be?"

Iqbal was puzzled. "What kind of question is that? What do you mean? I just told you. I want to be a doctor."

The man took his feet off the desk and put his hand on his chin. While he stared at Iqbal closely, he slowly caressed a red and gold striped tie and spoke in such a smooth manner that it made Iqbal even more uncomfortable. "Is it *you* that wants to be a doctor. Do *you* desire to be a doctor? Do *you* dream day and night of helping people who are ill? Do *you* dream of helping your community? Who do *you* want to save? Who do *you* want to please?"

"That doesn't make sense," said Iqbal as he abruptly jumped up from his seat. "What are you talking about? I want to save people. People who are sick. Who do you think I want to save?"

The man leaned forward, smiled reservedly, and nodded his head. "I don't know. Only you know who you want to save. Just make sure it isn't just yourself."

"What is that supposed to mean?"

"It means what it means. Figure it out Mr. blue chip MCAT. Figure it out before you leave for medical school."

"I have figured it out," Iqbal said to himself. "I have figured it out, haven't I?"

• ❖ •

Shireen and Akbar Ahmed were born and married in Lahore. The wedding was covered in the society pages of the daily newspaper and people talked about it for weeks. The bride wore a red and green bead-studded shalwar khameez and the groom wore a crisp, white sherwani with a black wool vest. Their families were ecstatic. Shireen's family was ensconced in Lahore academia, and Ahmed's family owned the city's premiere shipping company: Manzil International Freight.

Shireen was introduced to Akbar by a family friend who brought the two together over tea in the university canteen. It was fate, the two thought. Both were pursuing degrees in the Economics and Finance program, both had dreams of earning an MBA at London University's College of Economics and both articulated a lifelong objective of eventually settling down in America—preferably New York.

Good family backgrounds. Good scholarship. Good looking. They were the perfect match. As Shireen's friends put henna on her hands and teased her about the upcoming Ni'kah, a serene smile passed over the bride-to-be's face. She saw Akbar's face in her mind and knew he was the right man. "He is perfect," she said to her girlfriends. "He is really my soul mate. This is so wonderful. I will be married, and I do not even have to change my last name since it is the same as Akbar's." Shireen's girlfriends agreed. It was wonderful luck indeed. A good sign, they added as they stuffed Shireen's mouth with a large square of buttery halva.

· ❖ ·

A year after their marriage, Shireen and Akbar moved to London. It was there that they completed their MBA's and decided to start a small accounting and finance firm. The client base would primarily be composed of import and export companies that had long standing shipping contracts with Manzil International Freight.

After looking at different office spaces in central London, Akbar decided to set up their firm in a modest townhouse near the British Museum. "It will be nice to be near a monument, a veritable landmark. We could tell clients that we're a stone's throw from the British Museum," he said to Shireen as he pointed to the location on a glossy map. "It's in the center of everything. I can't think of a better location."

Akbar specially ordered the door-plate at Harrod's. He and his wife both took turns hammering in the nails on the front door. It was solid silver, square and beautifully engraved. The sign read:

Ahmed & Ahmed Associates

Since its grand opening, there was a steady stream of clients being serviced at Ahmed & Ahmed Associates. The Ahmed's felt blessed. After a year, the business became more lucrative than either Shireen or Akbar could ever have imagined. As Akbar's family's shipping company expanded service to Kuwait, Saudi Arabia and the neighboring Persian Gulf region, more clients were referred to Ahmed & Ahmed Associates. Their success enabled them to purchase the adjacent townhouse as their residence.

"How absolutely convenient," Akbar said.

"Well, if we have the means, then why not? We can have our tea in the comfort of our own home and then stroll to the office," said Shireen as she smiled over a tray of expense account audits.

In 1974, Shireen and Akbar decided it was time to start a family. They had hired a small support staff so Shireen could work part-time and take leave if necessary.

Shireen was devoted to the business that she had helped build. She was tenacious. She decided not to take any time off and worked through her entire pregnancy. After all, she thought, what did she struggle so hard for in school. Why quit now while they were ahead, she told Akbar.

In the humid London summer of 1975, a son was born to the Ahmed's. At first, Akbar wanted to name their son Ahmed. Upon consideration, Shireen firmly advised against it. "Do you want our son's name to sound like an echo. Oh *Ahmed Ahmed,* sweet *Ahmed Ahmed,*" she teased. Shireen finally suggested to name their son after her favorite Urdu poet, Iqbal. Akbar was reluctant, calling to Shireen's attention that the name sounded "too soft", but later agreed when she insisted on the name.

Two years later, Iqbal was joined by a sister. The baby's name, Fairouz, was suggested by an up and coming employee of the Ahmed's who kept constant company with songs sung by an Egyptian chanteuse of the same name.

A crib and play area were designated in the office. Iqbal and Fairouz cried, ate, played and slept while calculators and computers juggled and crunched miles of dizzying numbers and balances in the offices of Ahmed and Ahmed Associates.

· ❖ ·

After six years in London, Akbar and Shireen made plans for the final leg of their journey. They would move their firm to New York City by the coming fall. Office space had been purchased in Manhattan and their London clients recommended the firm to business associates in New York.

Clients in New York informed the Ahmeds that there was a large community of Indian and Pakistani Muslims residing in an outer borough of the city called Queens. So it was decided: A house would be purchased in the Bayside section of Queens. It was better, the Ahmed's agreed, to stay close to one's countrymen.

The Ahmed's were jubilant. Their children would be reared in America. They would be successful in New York City, the Greatest City on Earth.

In New York, Shireen thought it would be best to leave the business in Ahmed's hands. He could handle it by himself. Her job now was to raise the children. This was a large city. There were things here that she had seen in London, but Iqbal and Fairouz were still babies back then. Now, they would go out into the world without her by their side. They needed her to guide them—to keep them on the path of success.

The relatives in Pakistan were overjoyed. The children's grandparents showed their neighbors photographs of their rosy cheeked grandchildren. After holding the photos in front of friends and neighbors for hours, Iqbal and Fairouz's grandparents always said, "These are our *American* grandchildren. Yes. They are being raised in the world's greatest country."

Shireen and Akbar decided that their children would not be sent to public school. They wanted something better for them. They wanted their children to socialize with children that came from a better class of people. After consulting with some of Akbar's clients, it was decided to send the children to a Catholic school.

"At least there we know the children will be taught by priests and nuns," said Akbar.

"Well, yes. That would be more decent. That would be safer. We did not come this far to have our children ruined," said Shireen.

"They say that private schools are better in New York. Better than the public schools. In public schools, who knows who Iqbal and Fairouz would be associating with."

"Yes, Akbar, you're right. It would be best."

The children were enrolled in Blessed Mary the Virgin Grammar School in Bayside, Queens. A yellow school bus honked its melodious horn outside the Ahmed's door each morning. Its side panels were painted with a blood-orange burning heart from whose core bursted the pale, glowing face of the Virgin underneath a golden halo throbbing with light. Iqbal and Fairouz ran inside the bus to join other children wearing expertly cut navy wool blazers embroidered with a bright yellow cross on the chest pocket.

• ❖ •

On Sundays, Iqbal and Fairouz were sent to Islamic Weekend School. They hated waking up so early on Sunday mornings, but their parents thought it would be good if they could at least read the Qur'an. Sunday School wasn't like real school, the children thought. There were no uniforms and the kids just ran all around the place while adults lumbered about hollering at them in Urdu. Iqbal did not like to wear his shalwar khameez to Qur'an class. The shalwar was so baggy and had a stupid string at the waist that always got knotted up. Fairouz did not understand why she just couldn't wear the plaid skirt that she wore to real school. And what about that dumb dupatta that she had to wear on her head. It was silky and see through and kept slipping off her head. What good was that? What was it for anyway?

Every last Saturday of the month, Shireen and Akbar took their children to a community pot-luck dinner held in the basement of the Islamic Weekend School building. Over chicken khorma, biryanee and warm nans, the Ahmeds mingled with other families in the community. Akbar liked talking about his business and Pakistani politics over dinner. In the Brothers' Section, men congregated in identifiable cliques. The doctors, engineers, accountants, academics and businessmen sat in one circle. The newly arrived immigrants, cigarette and candy store owners, taxi drivers, restaurant workers and domestic laborers sat in another.

Once in a while the two groups mingled, but only to be separated when discussions led to the topic of whether or not one had a house or was forced to reside in a measly apartment. If the Imam or Hafiz was present during the dinners, then the two cliques managed to sit together for a short while. But one thing was always bound to happen: discussion would begin about family back home. For those who had come to his country to escape poverty, bad families, or stigmatized status, the discussion was a signal to leave. One could not discuss one's family back home if it were the very reason one left in the first place. And whether one was here as a "legal" was another story. So ultimately, the groups sat in the same room but on two separate islands.

The newly arrived understood that class lines were going to be drawn in their beloved America as well. The successful brothers were the first ones to put that policy into effect. What could one do? If you were not good enough to know back home, then obviously you would not be sitting in their circles in America either.

"Business is good," Akbar said. "Shireen stays home with the children, so I know that they are safe. Iqbal and Fairouz go to a private Catholic school in Bayside. They are with a better class of children. You know how it is here."

"Oh, you're lucky," Mr. Rizak concurred. "You know, most of the public schools are quite bad. At least you can be confident that your children are learning, that they are being educated."

"How is your Abdullah doing?" asked Akbar.

Mr. Rizak's eyes lit up. "Abdullah is very happy at his new school in Manhasset. He always says to me, 'Dad, I have it all: football, cheerleaders, tutors, games.' He is quite happy.

He told his mother and I the other day that he has decided to be a cardiologist. We always expected him to be a neurologist, but we can compromise, I suppose. We just signed him up for PSAT prep. It's never too early, you know. His mother wants him to make a speech next month to the children here at the Weekend School about medical careers. She says he could inspire the children with his attitude."

"It's good that we can send the children to Weekend School," Mr. Raoof said. "They can learn how to read the Qur'an; they have a place to go for Eid, and they can mingle with other good Muslim children. These children do not know how easy they have it in America. We had to struggle. They have every opportunity for success. You watch, in ten years each and every one of these kids will be lawyers, doctors or engineers. It's a given. These are some lucky kids."

As Akbar socialized in the Brothers' Section, Shireen sat on floral sheets spread on the floor of a classroom designated as the Sisters' Section and talked with the women.

The women, unlike the men, did not sit in overt cliques. In the Sisters' Section, one's economic and social standing was easily determined by gaze. Gaze was the subtext of affiliation and the sugar of chosen friendships. You did not have to ask. You simply saw with your own eyes whose stylish handbag's price could pay half your rent. You looked, but you did not say a word. You did your best and kept up with the conversation. If the sisters did not think that you, of all people, had anything interesting to say, then you heard the signifying chorus: a slight coughing followed by the dainty clearing of eleven uninterested throats (as though the women's windpipes were lodged with a very small piece of your boring comment), *"Ahem, ahem, right, uh-huh, anyway, as I was saying..."*

You understood, you did not need an explanation. A sister had bossed you into a corner while the other sisters did nothing. So you remained silent for the rest of the night because you did not want to make a scene. Your cheeks turned red and your head felt heavy. It wasn't worth the energy, you thought. Anyway, why be like them. If one sat near pigs, one did not have to put one's foot in the mud and get dirty as well. If you were fortunate, another sister—who understood—came to sit by your side. If you weren't, then you sat alone and remained silent until it was time to get your empty pot and go home. You were thankful for small blessings: At least your character remained intact.

If the women had something to say about someone else, if they thought Diba's khameez was a bit too tight, if Sa'ba talked too much about her children's grades, if Sonyah spoke a bit *too* intelligently, or if Jameela looked at Farida in a rude way when she asked for another serving of biryanee, then they called their friends the next day and dissected the evening over the phone.

If a sister did not like what she saw, if she wanted to follow the Sunnah, then she prayed that her sisters would be blessed with some sincerity and proper adhab and hopefully grow a real backbone by the next pot-luck dinner.

"We are planning to move to Long Island," said Mrs. Kareem. "Sohail's business is doing very well, and it's time we moved the children into a house of their own."

"Yes, we moved to the Island last year," commented Mrs. Rizak. "There are so many facilities there like malls, great private schools and pools for the children. There are so many good Pakistani families in the area as well. Some even have connections to politics."

"Oh yes," added Mrs. Raoof," I really like it there. And you know, we just remodeled the basement of our house so Ali could move his practice right downstairs. Now I just walk down the stairs to bring him lunch. He is right there. It is so convenient. And it isn't far away from Queens. We can still bring Sadia and Afzal to Sunday School. It's just thirty minutes on the Southern State Parkway."

"Yes, it is convenient," agreed Mrs. Rizak as she spooned some firnee into her mouth. "Abdullah says that the children are nicer in his school in Manhasset than they were at his school here in Queens. He is always at one friend's house or another. They are always playing those video games. They play for hours at a time. I really don't understand. But we are just happy to know that he is safe. When he is ready to come home, he calls me and I go pick him up. He will get his license by the fall, so we are getting ready for it. Jameel jokes with me and says that I better get ready for some dents on the Lexus."

While their parents engaged in conversation in the basement, Iqbal and Fairouz sat with the other children on the first floor of the Masjid hall.

"My parents bought me a Sega," Abdullah said.

"Well, so what. My parents bought me a Sega, silver Oakleys *and* a snow board because I got the top Math and Science scores on the Regents," shouted Afzal as he poked Abdullah in the stomach.

"Big deal!" interrupted Iqbal. "You guys go to stupid public schools and so what if they are in Long Island—they're still public. So that's easy. I go to a private school, and I was selected as Senior Leader and School Senator. They even selected me as Boy Leader for noon Mass next Friday. I'm going to be giving a little speech after Mass."

"Mass! What the heck is that? Isn't that like Catholic? You go to Mass? That's like haram, right? I mean, like don't Catholics believe that Prophet Isa is God *and* God's son? Explain that one to me. Man, that's messed up big time," said Qasim.

"What do you mean about it being haram?" asked Fairouz as she put both hands on her hip and pointed to Qasim. "Explain *that one* to me!"

"Haram means like unlawful in Arabic. It's the opposite of halal, little miss genius. So what part of unlawful do you *not* understand?" said Qasim waving his finger in the air.

Fairouz rolled her eyes at the boys and started to yell, "We aren't doing anything unlawful! Our parents said it was okay! My brother is smarter than all of you losers put together. You're all just jealous. You wish you could go to a nice school and wear nice uniforms. You wish you could make a speech in front of all your friends!"

"No, we don't," retorted Qasim and Abdullah, their voices cracking in unison.

"Who cares what stupid private school you go to since we're all going to end up in Stuyvesant or Bronx Science, or Brooklyn Tech if you're a wannabe. So what!" yelled Afzal.

"Yeah," said Sadia, who started to laugh heartily at the boys. "Who cares about losers anyway. My parents say that I'm going to be a doctor. They're buying me a car when I get into medical school. We'll see which one of you losers actually gets into medical school. And we'll see who'll be driving some nasty used car. Right Iqbal?"

"Oh shut up, Sadia," said Iqbal as he shoved his kufi in his pocket.

• ❖ •

Six years later, Iqbal sat at the kitchen table examining his MCAT scores for the forty-ninth time. He thought about what the man said in the dream. He still couldn't figure it out.

Shireen looked at her son and smiled. Her boy was finally on his way to become a doctor. "Do you think the score will get higher if you stare at the paper," laughed Shireen.

"That's funny, Mom," said Iqbal as he stirred his coffee. "Real funny."

"Well, look, your father and I are satisfied. We're going to have a doctor in the family."

"I know," Iqbal droned. "Right. A doctor in the family."

"I told the Kareems and Raoofs about your scores. They were so jealous. I think that you got a higher score than Sadia and Afzal. But you know, we knew that all along. Mr. Raoof was bragging to your father about Sadia's new car. As if we even cared."

"Whatever, Mom."

"What do you mean, 'Whatever'," said Mr. Ahmed as he walked into the kitchen. "That is no way to talk to your mother. What is wrong with you today?"

"Listen, I'm sorry, I don't mean to be rude. I'm just feeling...a little weird, that's all."

"Weird? What is that? Why should you feel weird?"

"*I* shouldn't feel weird? I know. I know. I should feel

fine, right?. Happy, right? But I just do. I just do. I just feel different. I just. I just..."

"You just what? What?" questioned Akbar as he looked at Iqbal with thick, furrowed brows.

Iqbal put his head in his hands and pressed his temples. "I don't know. I mean, I thought that I had always wanted to go to medical school. I mean that's all you and Mom have been talking about since grammar school. You always said, Iqbal, you will be a doctor. We need a doctor in the family."

"Iqbal, if you're trying to say that we forced you..." whispered Shireen with her left hand clutching her heart.

"I'm not trying to say anything. It was just, like, *expected*. And I did well. I liked science. I liked a lot of things in college. Being on the newspaper was great. Tutoring the kids in the prep program was fulfilling. Biology was great too, but med school was like going to determine the family's honor or something. You always said, 'Iqbal and Fairouz will be doctors. They will be doctors. Two doctors in the family...' blah blah blah. That's all I've heard. I don't know now. I don't know."

"You don't know what?" asked Mr. Ahmed as he leaned over Iqbal with both fists on the kitchen table. "What is it that you don't know? You don't know how hard we've worked. You don't know how much we've invested in private schools, how much we tried to build you up in the community. Your mother stayed home. She has an MBA, or did you forget that? She gave up her career so she could help you and Fairouz with your school work, go to school meetings, and pick you up from afterschool programs. She even took you to Manhattan, to the main library, whenever you wanted. She chauffeured you to review classes; do you remember that? How much garbage do you think I had to put up with just to maintain our status. The Ahmed's are not 'Whatever'. We know what we want. You better figure it out, son. You better figure out soon."

Akbar left the kitchen with a forehead wrinkled by fury.

Shireen, rendered frozen by her son's indecision, could not find her voice. She nodded her head while silently looking out through the sliding doors which led to the deck. That's where she planned to have Iqbal's graduation party. That's where her son would stand as he blew the candles off a cake which read, "Congratulations to our Future Doctor" in thick blue-gel frosting. A strawberry and pineapple cake that she had already placed on special order at Marietta's Bakery on Bell Boulevard.

Iqbal sat still, his eyes swollen with tears at the heavy glass dining table. He rubbed his eyes and placed his head in his hands. He felt like he was twelve, and his father had just torn up his algebra exam. He remembered exactly what his father said, "96%? You got a 96%? What kind of score is that? Where are the other four points young man? I suggest that you find them on the next exam. Do you hear me?"

· ❖ ·

Akbar felt the last twenty-one years of his son's life in his throat. "I don't believe this", he repeated over and over to himself as he stormed down the steps to the family room in the basement.

Shireen came down after a few minutes and watched him with a frown. Too consumed with changing the channels with the remote control, he did not even notice his wife's presence at the edge of the sofa until he looked up from the flurry of images that zoomed by his eyes.

Akbar looked at his wife silently. She helped me raise this ingrate boy of mine, he thought. "I don't understand, Shireen. I don't understand," he said as though he were trying to swallow an anvil before allowing his eyes to return to the glare of an infomercial on the screen.

Shireen shifted in her seat and wiped the perspiration from her upper lip. "Let's just look at this rationally. Alright? Maybe he's just a little confused. We know how sensitive he is. Maybe he's just a little nervous. Maybe he needs an hour or two to relax and sort it out. He is just nervous."

"Nervous? What does he have to be nervous about?" said Akbar as he banged the remote control on an end table.

"He has his scores in his hand. What has he been preparing for the last four years?"

"Akbar, don't get mad at me. I'm just saying that his head needs to clear."

"So what happens if it doesn't clear? What if he changes his mind?"

"Oh please, Akbar. Don't even think that way. He will come around. Give him an hour or two. We can all go out to lunch together. We can go to the Olive Garden near the mall. He loves the ravioli. He will eat a little, think and then he'll be back to the Iqbal we know. The tension will go down, and he will just admit that he wasn't thinking straight. It happens, Akbar. He's young. He's only twenty-one. It's just his mood right now. He has a lot on his mind."

"I don't know. I don't need this aggravation. We gave him the best."

Shireen took deep breaths and clutched her knees. "I know, I know. He knows that, too."

"Well, all I know is that Mr. Akbar Ahmed's son will be a doctor. That's what he has been prepared to do. That's what we expect. You can't just go through life and do what *you* want to do and act as though you have no responsibility to make your parents proud—to make them happy. I don't know how these kids think these days. Just bouncing from one interest to another. As if it is okay to just change one's course of life after a month or so. Don't these kids think about what they owe their parents? Don't they have any sense of honor? Of giving back? Who does he think brought him here? Who paid his tuition? Who put the money down for his dorm fees, for his plane tickets to and from college? Who paid for Stanley Kaplan and Princeton Review? Does he think he's just entitled to these things? He is doing no one a favor except himself. And what effect will this have on Fairouz? What will she do, Shireen, now that she sees her brother just throwing his life away because he suddenly feels weird?"

"Akbar, don't get ahead of yourself. Just calm down. We raised both our children in the best way possible."

Akbar stared at Shireen coldly. "Don't tell me that I'm getting ahead of myself. What? Are you on his side, too? You're the one who named him after that Urdu poet. Maybe he's just getting a little *poetic*, Shireen. See! Now look at what has happened. I don't want a sensitive son. I want a winner. A doctor. There is no room in my house for soft minds. I want a leader. I want a son I can hold in front of our family, our friends, and say: This is *my son* Dr. Iqbal Ahmed. There is no room in this house for the weak. What does he want to do, sell newspapers and candy? Write a little column in a newspaper? Sit with little children and teach them the alphabet? What a bloody joke."

Suddenly they heard a shattering noise from upstairs.

Akbar quickly threw the remote control aside and ran towards the stairs. "What has that boy done now!"

Shireen ran toward Akbar. "Oh no! Hurry, Akbar! Hurry!"

When they reached the kitchen Iqbal was no longer there. They scanned their eyes around the room. The sliding doors that led to the deck were locked. The coffee machine light was glowing red. Breakfast dishes were still stacked in the sink. No drawers were open. All the knives were accounted for. All eight, stood like steel sentries in the slots of the butcher rack. So they headed to the dining area.

From the kitchen, the corner of the glass dining table looked wet. It wasn't broken, Akbar was relieved. As they walked into the dining room, they noticed that the crystal swan centerpiece stood within a huge puddle of coffee on the surface of the table. When they looked up, they noticed a huge stain on the wall and broken pieces of a white ceramic mug on the area rug underneath the buffet.

"Of course. Of course he has to do it this way!" Akbar hollered. "I can't believe this boy! You would think that by twenty-one he would have half a brain."

Shireen covered her mouth. "I don't believe this! I don't believe this! He knew that I just had that wallpaper put up four weeks ago."

"He has lost his mind! He has really lost his mind! This is inexcusable. Where is he! Where is he!" Akbar yelled at Shireen as he swiftly kicked a leg of the maple buffet and headed toward the stairs.

"Sit down Akbar! Please! Stop it!" Shireen yelled in shock. "Don't go up there while you're still angry. Go get a glass of water. Sit down. He probably didn't mean to do it. He's never done anything like this before. Akbar!"

· ❖ ·

Iqbal knew that he shouldn't have thrown the mug against the wall. Mom would probably be upset about the stain, he thought. And Dad? Dad would be furious, of course. He knew that he felt tired of thinking about what other people wanted. His parents were nice people. His father was right. They did the best they could. Iqbal was not complaining, and that, he believed, was what his parents did not understand. He wasn't trying to insult them. He wasn't trying to step all over *their* dream. But in the end it was *their* dream, not his. He knew that he loved them. That he thought all about what could happen if he didn't do what they said. But they had raised him to be independent—to believe that he was intelligent. For that, he was grateful.

The room started to spin and Iqbal's head throbbed harder and harder. He held on to a pillow which he clutched over his stomach. His eyes were heavy and his throat felt as though it swelled with each passing minute. His body felt lighter and lighter, like he was floating through his skin and stepping on a thousand rays of light...

Iqbal opened his eyes and saw that he was standing in a quiet hallway. It didn't smell in that antiseptic kind of way. It was different, friendlier. He knew the scent. It was a familiar smell he remembered from his grammar school classrooms. It was comforting, sort of like a cross between vanilla cake and freshly cut grass.

The hallway was wide. Wide enough to have rooms on either side. All the doors seemed like they were made for short people. There was a single window, the size of a magazine, on each door. It wasn't made of glass, though. It was made of plastic. Iqbal bent down and rapped his hand on some of the windows. He peeked inside, but there was no one there. He saw that the rooms were empty except for a large rug at the center, a small fireplace in the corner and thousands of children's drawings hanging from the walls. He heard the voices of little children coming from the end of the hallway. He heard small, light footsteps and laughter.

As he walked to the end of the hallway, Iqbal smiled. He finally realized what the scent was. I should've known it before, he thought. It's crayons. Crayons! I smell crayons.

The scent filled Iqbal's lungs. He felt soothed. Safe. He felt like he was a kid again sitting at a short plastic table dipping his hands in a cookie tin and grabbing thick, colorful crayons. It was magic. You could make anything you wanted.

He remembered drawing purple dragons and stealthy black and red spaceships. At home, he remembered fighting for the gold and silver crayons with Fairouz (they ended up breaking them in half and taking turns with the copper).

As he walked to the end of the hallway, Iqbal started to feel cold. He zipped his fleece jacket all the way to his neck. But his hands and feet were still cold. When he looked down, he realized that he had no shoes or socks on his feet. Not to worry, he thought, there will be a fireplace in that room up ahead.

As he got closer to the door, the voices started to quiet down. He couldn't tell how many people were in the room. It sounded like five or six, but when he bent down to look through the window, he only saw the outline of one person, a young boy it looked like.

The door was unlocked, but it was about as tall as Iqbal's waist. So in order to go in, he had to get on his knees. Iqbal squeezed through the door carefully so as not to bang his head. Upon entering, he saw that this room looked just like the others. The fireplace glowed with a small fire and a bright green rug, a Salat rug, was spread in the center. There were no windows or cement walls. The walls were made of those small glass cubes and there was no ceiling. There was a clear blue sky that hovered above him.

"Assalamu Alaikum," a small, gentle voice called out. "Iqbal, come sit with me."

Iqbal turned around and saw that a small boy had suddenly appeared on the bright green Salat rug in the center of the room. The boy held out his right hand and pointed to the place in front of him.

As he walked toward the boy, Iqbal noticed that he, too, like the man in his dream, looked familiar. The boy smiled and stood up when Iqbal approached. He shook Iqbal's hand and hugged him whole-heartedly.

The boy looked up, stared directly into Iqbal's eyes and started to weep quietly. "I've been waiting for you, Iqbal," he said softly. "You finally came. It was a long time. But I knew you would come. There is so much to tell you before you go. There is so much you already know. You know yourself. Come and sit down here, Iqbal. Sit by me."

· ❖ ·

Akbar stood outside his son's bedroom door and took two breaths. With one hand on the doorknob and the other on his heart, he rolled his eyes and yelled at the top of his lungs. "Iqbal, you're going to give me a heart attack! Are you in there? Can you hear me? Open the door, boy! Open it now! Be a man and let your father in! You're big enough to throw things boy, right? You're big enough for that. Now open this door and stand up to me like a man!"

Iqbal slowly opened his eyes to the sound of wild knocking. Oh great, he thought. Don't worry the standoff has ended. He looked outside his window. It was about noon and the sun was shining bright as ever outside the window. He looked at his hands. They were warm and sweaty. He shifted under his blanket and banged his feet on the wooden foot board. He looked down to see that he had fallen asleep with his shoes on.

Akbar banged harder and harder. "Iqbal Ahmed, open the door NOW!"

"The door is open, Dad. I didn't lock it."

Akbar pushed in the door and stared at his son who sat up on a rumpled bed with shoes still on his feet.

"Don't you take your shoes off before you nap?" Akbar said as he stared at his son's worn sneakers.

"Yes, usually I do. I just forgot this time."

"You know, there's no excuse for throwing something in my house. You know, your mother is down there cleaning it up."

Iqbal rubbed his eyes. "I know Dad. I'm sorry. It was a stupid thing to do. It was just... impulsive."

Ahmed banged his hand on his son's desk. "Impulsive? Don't use those stupid psychological words with me. An Ahmed is not impulsive. Look at me son, tell me what you see."

"I see my Dad."

"What else do you see?"

"I don't know. Are you okay, Dad? Is this like one of your tests?"

"You see a successful man, don't you?"

"I guess so."

"What do mean you 'guess so.' "

Iqbal shifted uneasily and stared at his father. "I don't mean anything."

"You know, you put your Mom and I through a lot of stress today. It just isn't right. You can't just turn on your parents like that. No one will take care of you like your mother and I. You think it was easy? Huh? Well, it wasn't. You will understand one day when you have your own family...when you have your own children. It wasn't easy for me, and it won't be easy for you."

Iqbal looked at his father apologetically. "I know, I know, Dad."

"No, you don't know!" responded Akbar as he wiped the sweat from his forehead with a cotton handkerchief. "You just walk into a room and destroy what your Mom and I have been working towards for the last twenty-one years. You don't know anything. This world is for the successful. For the successful, you hear me!"

"Dad, I know that and I know what I want. I finally know what I want to do. It has been driving me crazy for the last two weeks. I can't even sleep right. But now I know. I know."

"You don't know anything, boy! You want to hurt us, right? Hurt the people who made all sorts of sacrifices for you. That's the way it is, right? That's what you've learned in the last twenty-one years."

Iqbal got out of bed and stood in front of his father. He brushed some hair off his face and straightened out his shirt. "I don't want to hurt you, Dad. I don't want to hurt anyone."

Akbar turned to his son. He covered his ears with his hand and nodded his head. "I don't want to hear it. The son we love will be a doctor. That's the end of the conversation. Now go wash your face and change your clothes. Your Mom and I are taking you out to lunch. Go on, get dressed. Be down in five minutes."

Iqbal turned around to say something before his father closed the door behind him, but he knew it wasn't the right time. It would have to wait. He remembered what the little boy said and for the first time in his life he knew exactly what he had to do.

"No amount of knowledge
or faith can benefit anyone
who does not know who they are."
- Sahih Hadith

Professionals

❖❖❖

"And when the rivers will be drained away
And when (various) people will be united together,
And when the girl-child who was buried alive will be asked:
For what offense was she killed."
- Qur'an 81:6-9

In a motel nineteen miles from seven lanes of pollution blackened toll booths and a glorious wing-like bridge, a boy orders his girl to push.

"Push hard and get this thing over with. We have to get back and study for mid-terms."

A few miles away, their chino and cashmere clad brethren toil away on campus. Over there, among manicured quads and shiny pink granite outdoor tiling, there are few issues which shock. Those who make it that far by money alone have the clout to conceal; therefore, shock is not of the essence. Damage control is part of one's mantra, and one never confuses emotion with adjustment. When one's family name is inscribed on towering library walls, then one has surely arrived. When the economy of lineage exempts one from sin, then one can surely laugh at that common, dirty horde of folk whose knuckles are bloody from just the struggle itself.

• ❖ •

The girl can't see any more. Everything is blurry.

The TV is on real loud, so the people in the next room don't hear the future dripping slowly on green linoleum twenty-four feet above pure Upstate asphalt. She wants to hurry, too. All she smells is coffee, soap and blood.

She tells him to move her Nine West mules to the side. "They're vachetta leather," she whines.

"Look, who cares about your stupid shoes. Just shut up and push."

The girl frowns like a fourth grader who just scuffed a pair of perfect white Keds. "I don't know why we didn't listen to the lady at the clinic and just do this the other way."

"That would be too problematic. Plus, I didn't want to do this during spring break."

He told me that all we had to do was pay for everything in cash and get it done and over with.

"It's not like we're on welfare," he said. "We aren't like that at all. We're the children of highly educated professionals. And anyway, listen, I don't think you want us to max out the cards. Cause you know why? Spring break is only two weeks away, remember? Relax."

Oh, yeah, the cards. He always thought about things like that. He also said we had to do this thing prepared. It's not like we're stupid people. It's nothing, really. Don't make it a bigger deal than it really is. I mean, it's not like our fault or anything. We're just taking care of things.

"Listen, it's no big deal," he said. "Just don't tell anyone. Act normal. It's not like no one has ever done it this way before. I mean, c'mon. Dad just got me my Jetta. Life's good. I didn't get my scholarship so I could end up in this disgusting motel. I don't come from that kind of family. I don't need any changes. Do you want to change things between us?"

"No."

"We'll forget about it after a week or two. You'll still have your 3.8, and I'll have my DAT scores in my hand. And we'll still have two tickets to Cancun."

"You promise, right? she answered. "I mean the girls in the house don't even know. They just think I've been overloading on Cherry Garcia during all-nighters. Isn't that funny? I mean, I have my outfits all picked out. You know, I showed them to you. I'll just have to lose the weight. Right?"

"Look, we'll be okay. Everything will get back to normal. Just like it was."

• ❖ •

A guy in chem lab told him about this motel. He told him they didn't care about anything. All we needed was a credit card. All we had to do was go prepared. It's all about us, he said. Us. It has nothing to do with It.

We pulled up here at about 2 a.m. The clerk was in his bathrobe watching videos in the office. He didn't even blink an eye when we signed in as Mr. and Mrs. Doe.

Before we crossed the bridge, we had gone to Kmart to get some garbage bags, paper towels, cleanser, sponges, rope, Advil and two boxes of Stayfree. He got mad at me when I told him to go back in for a copy of Vogue and a Twix.

Don't waste time. Be prepared. Get back to studying for midterms. Like clockwork he said. Anyway, stupid people don't get full scholarships.

"Everything will be fine," the boy pants in between running to the bathroom and changing his sweat drenched denim shirt.

"Are you sure?" she asks.

"Yeah, of course. It'll be like nothing happened, okay. Look, when we get down to Cancun for spring break, you won't remember a thing."

• ❖ •

It started coming in lecture hall. I just thought it was my fourth coffee of the day. But it wasn't. It was coming, that's all. I got up, dropped my bag by mistake and left. After I got outside to the quad, I realized that I left my copy of Plato's Republic on the seat next to me.

Then I beeped him. He came running from North Campus. He told me to relax while he cleaned up. I played some CD's and took some Advil. It was no big deal. It was just like real bad cramps, like the ones I used to get in junior high. That's when I used to leave school early and take about eight Pamprins and buy a bag of chocolate kisses on the way home. When I woke up, there were tiny balls of foil sprinkled like stars all over the carpet. There was a shiny path leading half-way to the window. From the window high above the street, I knew the day was behind me and everything would be okay.

· ❖ ·

Some movie with Molly Ringwald is flashing on the screen. Red hair, good teeth, nice clothes. I remember liking the soundtrack when I saw it on cable last year. I'm going to have to remember to bring some Sun-In with me to Mexico. Oh yeah, and some good CD's.

"C'mon, concentrate. I don't want to be here until tomorrow."

I wish he would stop screaming at me because it's not like It's inside him yanking with claws to get out. I mean, he didn't have to hide It from his mother. He didn't have to hide It from eleven girls with perfect cuticles. For me, it's been men's sweatshirts with layers of oversized plaid shirts and cargo pants for the last nine months.

She tells him she's cold. Freezing. The air conditioner is on high even though it's 40 degrees outside. "It feels like a darn meat locker in here," she says.

"Don't act like a child. I don't need that right now," he says. "And anyway, the cold air will keep the smell down."

· ❖ ·

It's about 1 p.m. The people next door just left. The winter sun is piercing through the pea green curtains. I feel like I'm inside the belly of a green, smelly thing. It's been eleven hours since we signed in. It hasn't arrived yet.

There's a knock on the door. Cleaning Lady in a torn Metallica T-shirt and red jeans stands outside the door blowing on her hands.

The boy yells at her to come back later. He pushes a twenty through the slit in the door.

No problem, she says in between hiccups. She can just go across the street and have a smoke until they're ready.

Don't tell the boss, she says.

"No problem," the boy whispers through the slit. "That's a small request."

Then It comes. I want It to go away. In the movies they always act like this part hurts with no end. I just feel hot, that's all. It's nothing worse than cramps or stomach rumbling after you vomit. He cuts the cord with a camping knife. It's crying and squirming. It's dirty with blood and sticky membrane. He's yelling at It. I only see the back of It's head. Wet, noisy, ugly creature.

A quick crack and the rapid crinkle of plastic.

He tells me to wait until he comes back. He goes out back to the dumpster.

I slide back into sheets that feel like jelly and thorns. My body doesn't feel anything except a gaping absence. As though miles of fossilized rope have finally unraveled and are being pulled from the center of my throat. I touch the mess to make sure I'm still here.

The room is no longer a room. I have fallen into a dark pit filled with snakes, dragons and scaly insects who are rank with urban odor.

I am not a dirty person.

I do not smell.

This is not my mess.

*He comes back and tells me to shower while he wipes up
the liquid and rolls up the sheets.*

"It'll be like we weren't even here," the boy yells to the
girl through the steady hiss of steaming water. "Hey, don't
take too long in there, okay."

*I don't want the water to stop. It's warm like the sprinkler
in the park behind our house. I just want to feel like myself again.
This has been for nothing. A waste of time. For nothing.*

"Hey, c'mon. Finish up already," the boy yells.

The girl turns off the tap and pulls the shower curtain
aside. As she watches the last bit of water slide over her feet,
she thinks she sees two small eyes peering from inside the
drain.

*I'm stupid. Just seeing things. Don't be a baby. Just put
on your clothes and get out of here. You didn't see anything. Don't
turn around again. There's nothing there.*

"Who were you talking to in there?" the boy asks with
a smirk on his face.

"Talking?" she asks. "I wasn't talking. The water just
wasn't going down. Forget it."

"Well, stop acting weird then and get dressed. I want to be out of here in a half an hour."

· ❖ ·

Forty-five minutes later we walk towards the Jetta. The ski racks up top catch the sun so hard that it almost blinds me. They glow red. Pointy racks burn my eyes. A crown of fire breaks the darkness when I close my eyes to blink. The inside of my mouth is burning. I quickly wipe the side of my mouth with a sleeve. There's something on my shoes.

The girl bends down to scrape something hard and red off her shoes. She gets up slowly because she feels dizzy. She smears some Blistex on her lips.

The boy stares at her shoes. He takes a look around the parking lot and tells her to stop.

"Give me the shoes!" he says while trying hard not to punch the wall on his side. We can't chance anything, alright!"

"What's wrong with you?" she says while rubbing her eyes. "Don't talk to me like that."

"Listen, I'm sorry, okay. Please. Just give them to me. Just be quiet and wait for me in the car."

He goes back to the dumpster. From the rearview, I see him coughing and spitting while he walks back to the car.

I flip the visor mirror. The light is soft. I look different. Tired. I look like my mother.

He slams the door. His upper lip is damp with sweat. He keeps on wiping his hands on his pants.

"It's over," the boy breathes. "Let's get out of here."

The sky flashes bright before sunset. In fifteen minutes we're gone; floating fast in the Jetta over the bridge. There are no clouds, and I can already see the skyline in the distance: sharp, clean, glistening spires.

I feel the rope being pulled from inside my throat.

He tells me to relax.

"Look, she's gone. We don't have any worries. Everything's back to normal now."

"She?"

"Yeah. Look forget it. It's over. We can wash our hands of this. No one knows about a thing. Listen, things without names don't exist. Forget it. It's just back to normal now. It's just you and me. Just you and me."

"I know, I know. It's just you and me."

I check my reflection in the visor mirror.

I look fine. Just a little powder, a little blush. I'll be fine.

I look out the window.

I feel clean.
This is not my mess.
There is no such thing as trouble.
Everything is normal. The way it used to be.
I fan my hand out the window to feel the wind.

The boy's brown eyes glow in a band of breaking light. "We're not like the others," he says softly.

"I know," the girl says as night and day disappear inside her head and tuck themselves between the terrifying comfort of momentary myths. "We're not like them. We're different. We come from a good family. Our parents are educated. We come from a family of professionals."

· ❖ ·

Little She takes her place amongst sheets soiled with blood and once soft shoes of leather hardened by droppings of afterbirth.

She is silently enthroned upon a dirty garden full of motel refuse, membrane and ash. Buttersoft skin, propped up by black plastic and rusty dumpster walls, shines by the first light of sunset which falls discreetly like a veil of lilac rain.

She, who is the size of two palms linked in prayer, takes her title at this selected hour with grace. She is illuminated, bathed in bursts of seashell blue and pollen yellow: Queen of the Unseen. Her winged scribes have come to settle upon her shoulders while a white car crowned with scalloped plastic and steel horns zooms away. Soon, it will cross a silver bridge, anonymous to naked eyes. Briefly, for a moment, it will be suspended in the distance. Attached like a magnet to a laced barbed wire train draped against a scarlet sky.

Carefully, the scribes sponge her body clean with rose oil and water.

Slowly, they fold her within layers of the most supple linen.

They ask, light inside voice, "For what crime was she killed?"

They are told to purify and no more.

Prayers are blown in each ear while tiny hands grasp even tinier wings.

A journey to a place of gardens with rivers flowing underneath and open Arms awaits her. In that place, fluttering ranks of perfumed green birds await her company. They have been told she will be with them soon. They rejoice; she is welcome; they will be waiting.

The scribes will deposit their parchment scrolls at the gate and walk with her, wings holding hands, to the light of a million suns and stars.

In that place, she already has a name.

"And no soul share bear the sin of another."
-Qur'an 35:18

Dear Teacher

❖❖❖

Dear teacher,

There is a quiet girl in your first grade class. She sits in row five, and you may not have really noticed her because she is very shy. She doesn't talk very much, although I'm quite sure there is nothing wrong with that. Some children, as you may have experienced, are silent by nature. They are blessed in other ways, perhaps they are artists or poets. Or maybe they enjoy literature and love to collect small leaves, stones and shells. I'm sure you've seen all kinds of children in your tenure as a teacher. It is a blessed vocation, teaching, quite trying as well, I'm sure.

This girl, the one I mentioned before, the one who sits quietly in your class, is my daughter. You may have forgotten her name, and that is quite alright. It is only the fifth week of class. Her name is Nusaybah. Yes, it is a unique name. A name most often mispronounced by her teachers and classmates. The children, and even you, perhaps, call her 'No-Say-Baa', as though demanding a small girl not to imitate the sound of sheep.

For my husband and myself, and for our daughter's grandparents, Nusaybah's name is like a song. Like something the wind disclosed in secret while I lay fast asleep in my eighth month of pregnancy. Sometimes my daughter's name sounds like the voice of the ocean, like the rhythm of echoes through a wave. But there is one thing that is important for you to know, maybe something you could share with your class: her name has nothing to do with sheep, and nothing to do with the noise or characteristic of any farm animal.

You may not know this, but my daughter is named after an important companion of Prophet Muhammad* named Nusaybah Umm-Imarah. (In case you aren't familiar with Prophet Muhammad*, he was last in a line of Prophets which include Abraham*, Moses*, Jesus* as well as others. Muslims refer to Prophet Muhammad* as the seal of the Prophets.)

When I named my daughter, I thought of this beautiful woman, Nusaybah Umm-Imarah. This brilliant soldier of Islam was present at the Battle of Uhud with her husband and sons. She was a woman who brought water to the injured. She carried a sword, a bow and a quiver of arrows, ready to defend herself against surprise attack as she tended to the wounds of fallen soldiers.

Nusaybah Umm-Imarah was one of the ten people to have composed the human shield which protected the Prophet* during the Battle of Uhud. In her sincere devotion to protect the Prophet*, she did not even see that her very own son lay wounded near her. The Prophet* saw him and said to her, "Bandage your wounded." And so she did. But being that she was so eager to defeat the enemy, as soon as she bandaged her son, she told him, "Rise and fight the enemy."

That is the story behind the name of the little girl that sits in row five of your classroom. She may not be able to articulate it yet, and you may not have come close enough to see it in her eyes, but she is a fighter. A fighter, I must clarify, in the more literary sense. She has, if you care to look, a strong, sensitive soul. She has, if given the chance, the ability to convey her ideas and thoughts to the other children in the class.

Children's minds at birth, as we learn in college, are *tabula rasa*. A blank slate, if you will, that is ready to take notes with the speed of a laser pen if given half the chance. In our adult world, it seems that we sometimes stain this slate with the wrong words and feelings. Adult graffiti splattered upon the psychological canvases of beings too young to inflict exclusion or harbor thoughts of hatred for their peers. It can happen in such subtle ways, in moments that are smaller than minutes themselves, but which simultaneously hold the power to damage the subject of the slander. At times, whether consciously or unconsciously, we may give our children the impression that it is alright to slander or ridicule a classmate's name and identity, that it is alright to ignore someone if they look, act, speak or dress differently from us. That's when the slate is broken or chipped slightly if we're lucky because then there is time for repair.

Nusaybah, like the other children in your class, was not born a victim. She neither requires special treatment, nor does she ask for special attention. But one thing that should be availed to her, and everyone else around us, is understanding. And the last time I made a general observation, it occurred to me that understanding is still free. One does not need to purchase it in the market. If one cares to look, it is available in bulk. Immeasurable yards of it can be found in the eyes of children. And yes, I do see it in my daughter's eyes, still.

Recently, I've noticed something strange. During the evenings, after Nusaybah has her bath, it has become somewhat of a habit, a ritual, to sit down and read a story before she goes to bed. Before she chooses her story, I usually ask her what happened in school, what she read and so forth. These days, when I ask her this question, she starts to cry. You see, she isn't the type of child who manipulates crying to her advantage. When she does cry, it is sincere and she tries to hide it with all her might.

I do not fault Nusaybah for her sensitivity; I admire her for it. I admire that at six years of age she has the ability to know how she feels, truthfully and without drama. She tells me that she doesn't like school anymore. As my daughter cries, she tells me about the stares and teasing that she gets from some of her classmates. Like, for example, when some of the children make fun of the way she wears pants underneath her dresses. I must help you to understand that we are Muslims, and we encourage our daughter to dress modestly. We aren't paranoid. We just don't want her dress riding up during school activities. That, of course, would be highly embarrassing. Nusaybah said that some of her classmates have also tried to pull her scarf off her head during class and recess. The scarf, which is known in Muslim culture as the *hijab*, is an Islamic requirement for girls who have reached puberty. Nusaybah has chosen to wear it now because she likes it. Her classmates should be encouraged to respect this right. She also disclosed to me that she feels bad that the teacher doesn't help her when the other children start laughing at her.

I know, I know, we mustn't intervene in the social interaction of children. But I must say that I'm alarmed. I don't send my child to school so that she can become the focal point of jokes and the scapegoat for classroom mischief. I used to send my child to school with the confidence that inclusion would be modeled and fostered by the teacher. That a child who dresses and speaks differently from other children would be given the chance to be understood. That the teacher would step in to encourage the other children to understand

and appreciate on their level how Nusaybah is different, and that she—like them—is still just a child.

Imagine how frightened you would be if everyone stared at you when you walked passed them. Imagine if the stares were coupled with laughter and whispers. Then imagine that you were six and relatively new to this country. Frightening, isn't it? That's what my daughter has been experiencing on a daily basis. But as I said, she was, after all, named in honor of a fighter. So that is what she will have to do: Fight to be perceived on one level only—the level of truth.

My daughter writes her thoughts in a little blue journal that her grandmother purchased for her as a gift when she started the first grade. Sometimes, after dinner, Nusaybah takes her journal out from her school bag and shows us what she has written. As you are not with us when we have our evening meal, let me share with you what she wrote on Tuesday:

'Today was a sunny day. The sky was blue and light. A bird sang. I think. I saw it sitting on the tree. The bird saw me. My teacher doesn't see me. I see me. I am not bad. The boys and girls laugh. They laugh at me. I feel sad. My teacher said talk loud. I do not talk loud. My teacher does not see me.'

At the age of four, Nusaybah began to read. Alphabets at first, after that small words, and then young children's books. She loved to read aloud to her grandparents. Like all parents, we thought our child was brilliant. She showed a real aptitude for reading and reciting the stories she had heard out loud. Last year, in kindergarten, Nusaybah was a finalist in the K-G Storytellers Contest. She spoke in a gentle voice because, as she told me after the contest, "I just want to tell the story, Mommy, I don't want to be loud." That was fine with me. She did her best.

My husband and I try to read with our daughter every day. She reads the Qur'an, in Arabic and English, quite well. And yes, she does read a bit softly. But I do not think that a low voice is "indicative of any dysfunction and/or learning disability" that you had so thoughtfully diagnosed in the comments section of last week's progress report.

I assure you that in Nusaybah's case vocal tone is not an issue related to cognition. In fact, I highly doubt there is an assessment instrument which could calibrate her "problem area." I don't think that sensitivity and the desire to be understood are a signs of cognitive weakness. I doubt if there is a tool out there which can determine or assess the "proper" level of sensitivity (or if there is a set of criteria for what quantifies proper sensitivity in the first place).

Quite frankly, every child has a right to be understood and a right to be *sensitive to* and *aware of* how others perceive them. In reference to the latter, if Nusaybah's classmates, and you, as her teacher, do not understand and perceive her as a "normal and competent" child, then the error of perception or understanding is *your* area of concern, *not hers*. Understanding is in the eyes of the beholder and, in this case, the beholder is in the position of power.

Nusaybah likes school. She likes reading, writing, sports and being with other children. But these days, she is just a little scared. It hurts me to see my daughter scared because she has always been fearless. Maybe I can be faulted for caring too much, but when has caring ever been something negative? I doubt if a parent can be guilty of caring too much.

I'm sure you must understand that it is not easy to wear one's identity on one's sleeve. At such a young age my daughter is dealing with the type of behavior that even some adults cannot face; behavior that challenges one's emotional strength and identity. And then there are those words. Words that she tries to explain and spell as best she can: *foreigner, scarf-head, terrorist-baby.*

The little girl that is in your class can only be who she is and no one else. She is a Muslim and has informed me that she wants to stay that way even if "the children and teacher have bad eyes at me."

As I stated, my daughter is a fighter, and we, her family, intend to support her as best we can. She has been encouraged to be independent, to fight her own battles. She understands that Mommy and Daddy can't step in and make it better all the time. But Mommy and Daddy do speak and read English, quite well in fact, and will not ignore her feelings or her teacher's comments. (No need to staple those ESL Classes for Adults flyers to her notebook each Friday.)

This morning, when we offered our early morning prayer, Nusaybah asked if she could make a special supplication at the end. Nusaybah asked *Allah* for one thing. She said, "Allah, please help me to still be a strong Muslim girl." (Allah is the Arabic word for God in pure form, pure light. Muslims believe that God does not exist in human form; he is not a man, not an eight-armed woman, nor a ghost. For Muslims, Allah is just God and nothing and no one else.)

My daughter has informed me that she wants to continue being a Muslim because she just wants to be who she is. She is saddened by what she experiences in her class, but she is not discouraged. Nusaybah will neither compromise, nor change her identity just because the people around her refuse to understand her way of life. But I do hope that you will at least try to understand her a bit better, and maybe you can give her some room to help her to understand you.

As I explained earlier, Nusaybah was named after a strong Muslim woman who fought as well as healed. If you create some space for understanding her, then your classroom will benefit from her fighting spirit as well as her profound sense of healing.

My daughter is still quite young, a child of six, but her soul is spacious and her mind is ever-expanding. In that aspect, she is not different from any other child in your class.

Children, by instinct, crave to understand the world around them. It wouldn't be fair to stand in the way of their understanding. Nor would it be fair to taint or skew that understanding—or filter it through adult biases.

If you stop for a moment, you will see that Nusaybah has already taught you something: That proliferating false perceptions does not make one as mighty as a mountain—it just pushes innocent and misunderstood people into very uncomfortable corners.

As you may well know, the very essence of a good teacher is the ability to continue learning from one's students. Nusaybah's faith allows her to have faith in others, and maybe that's something we can all learn from her.

Epilogue:
Vision Scribes

1
Cycles

Within families, there are private histories being written as the day moves on its predetermined schedule. As the moon and sun take orders, as the tide rushes in and takes its leave, as the stars mingle amongst friends and then fall quickly to smudge the sky with lines the color of rose water, children are born and families rejoice at the sight of little hands.

The angels, our invisible scribes, pick up their pens and scribble what they witness. Adhan is called in each ear and history is revised again.

Grandparents watch as a tiny part of themselves kicks little feet in the air. *Yes, that little one has a long way to go, Insha'allah. Let the child learn the names of things, let the child see with fresh vision what we have seen for ages.*

An open window blows flannel curtains over the child's crib. The child feels the message of the wind on a smooth face. The angels lick transparent forefingers, dip feathery quills in silky ink and turn to a clean page. The wind has conveyed the child's message to them. It must be written.

• ❖ •

2

On Nan'na's Time

I always saw my Nan'na in my mind as she appeared in black and white photographs taken in her youth. I saw her as a young woman, waking up on silent mornings, speaking with her mother over the circus of pots and pan and morning dough, dipping a soft piece of toast in warm, milky chai and combing the hair of younger sisters whose dresses she will have to hem for even younger ones on the way.

I did not know my Nan'na well enough to know about the specific details of her experience in this life, but I asked my parents, my aunts and uncles and cousins about her habits, loves and strengths. With their help, I attempted to piece together what she may have felt, touched, understood and experienced. It was important to me. I thought that to know *my* self, I had to know *her* self.

Once, I gathered enough courage to request my Nan'na to tell me about her life as a child, as a young woman and why she didn't remarry after my grandfather passed away. She squinted her black as burnt wicks eyebrows, squeezed my hands and laughed.

"Why would you want to know about that," she asked.

"I'm curious," I told her. "I want to know about you. I want to know if we have anything in common."

She smiled and told me about having to go to a well to get water and preparing food for her siblings and husband. She told me that she and her siblings had a private tutor that taught them how to read the Qur'an and how she took long walks by the seashore. She told me about getting married at fourteen and having seven children running around her before she was twenty-three. She told me about my Na'na Jan being her first and last love.

I still wanted to know more. A million questions were running through my mind. I wanted to know her every move as a child, as a young woman. I wanted to be able to trace back all her movements and thoughts so I could know her.

After a little while, she told me that she was tired of talking.

"You ask too many questions," she said. "Don't you get tired? Don't you want something to eat? A little roasted corn, some salty channa maybe?" She laughed before blowing on a steaming cup of chai.

"No," I said, "I'm not hungry, thank you. And no, Nan'na, I don't get tired of asking."

"But are you listening?" she asked. "Have you listened to what I have said? Because if you listened to the little that I have told you, then you know me. In fact, you will know me and yourself very well."

She finished her chai and told me she was going to the porch to take a short nap. She pulled my earlobe and told me that I needed a nap as well.

"No, Nan'na," I said, "I'm not that sleepy."

"Who's talking about sleeping," she said.

I took the cup from her hands, sipped the last drop clinging to the bottom and took my place besides soft, wrinkled feet that had just walked me right inside myself.

· ❖ ·

3

You Remember

Isn't it true that sometimes you take someone's hand and are led to places unknown? You are wide-eyed, breathless and you know that inside your heart is melting. It is not in defeat that your heart turns to liquid, but in affirmation that the unfamiliar will soon bind with what is inside.

You know what your mother told you. That what is inside you shall always work as talisman against all the violent wind, scorching sun and torrential rain that people and nature can afford to throw your way while reaching with greedy hands into deep, mysterious pockets.

"So go on," your mother said, "go ahead and look at people in their faces. What are you afraid of? I did not sweat all these years to raise daughters who cry at the sight of strangers. I gave my milk to daughters who will raise their fists at this world and wrap their arms, strong and hard, around their mother and father when they are done. Those are the kind of daughters I raised. I'll see what you can do with yours."

Isn't it true that no matter how much education you think you may have, you will never mumble a sentence that will outshine the wisdom that was uttered to you right before you left your house with your father's old wool coat flapping like the broken wings of a pathetic black-winged gull on your hips? Remember? That was right before you took that last spoonful of rice, secretly from your mother's plate, into your mouth. You didn't choke on it. You swallowed it. Hot, buttery, clean. She turned around and saw you. She smiled and arched eyebrows soft as midnight that said, "I know." You both laughed. She said that you and her were one and the same. No differences; just some misunderstandings. But nothing so deeply rooted in sorrow, wide with bitterness and gaping with dismal mood. Nothing that would keep your hearts aching, longing for comment, apart. Nothing that would make you hold the phone in a cold, indecisive hand for twenty minutes before dialing. It was nothing that couldn't be solved by sheer soul-force, a couple of friendly fists on a door or table and finally a couple of nods, knowing looks and a quick pat of tissue. All she said was "I know," and you knew the healing began there.

You listened carefully and looked at the way her hands moved your hair behind your ear. You grabbed her words like giant butterflies in your hands. You kept a thoughtful hold. You wrote them down on your palm that very minute. The ink was wet so you pressed your hand on a journal page and kissed the cover.

Her words were like kisses, blown soft and warm; fluttering and then folding in half like turquoise waves before they landed on your face. Her words were wisdom from a woman who ran into traffic to catch her daughter's winter hat. She was the one who told you that it was natural to be scared. She helped you to understand that after you did what you could, the only thing left to do was put it in His Hands.

She is the same woman now as she was then. The woman whose cardigan pockets were filled with candy and little flowers. Pockets you couldn't reach back then unless you stood on a dining room chair. She is the woman with an armor of grace who told you to embrace fear, soothe down your ruffled feathers, lick the tears and resuscitate yourself using the fires that lay inside. You cannot forget such words. Words that stroke themselves on your mind like relentless mink.

4

Witness

What will my hands say on Judgment Day? Will they speak about who they have touched, hands they held, papers torn three hours after sunrise? Or will they say that they did the best they could with what was known to them at the time. That I was cautious and sensitive. Or will they say that I constantly used them to rub the angry red out of my eyes, the scorn-filled faces out of my head. That I tried, tried very hard in fact, to keep my hands to myself.

Will my hands take off on their own? Belligerent, unguided, slow at first, then burst high into the flickering magenta of a dying sunset's flame? Or will they rest on a dirt covered rock, weary with the thought, that although they tried, they could not save everyone.

As I sit here now, my hands are trying to contain the conversation of my heart, and my feet throb and float on the memories of many journeys taken, of many houses that have been entered. My feet recall steps taken in anger, pure love and even guilt sometimes. They tell me about kicks of revenge shot sharp like staccato slices of the wind in the dark, kicks brief and hot like the monologue of kindling. My feet remind me of clumsy trips taken here and there which resulted in bruises, which opened my eyes and showed me the way.

Finally, my feet tell my heart that they remember the silky roll, the lovely music of lush grass, which felt like the fur of momentary secrets underfoot.

I know that although I would like to, I simply cannot speak for my hands and feet. For their voices are sealed until the proper time. But I can speak for myself, and I know what I will tell them. I will thank them for being kind to me, for being fair. That when the journey of this life is over, we will concur that mistakes were made, dishes were thrown in anger and the slap was a matter of honor—nothing else—and honor counts, doesn't it?

What about the rush? they will ask. *The rush to go here and there without logic, without reason. Remember the errors? Doors opening, your feet scurrying, not even a glance back, or a second look,* they will say.

I will try to speak softly to these two hands, these two feet, for they are my friends. I will tell them there were no errors at all. That they had, in fact, provided me with the two things I could never have provided for myself: a way to get up off the floor and a sure grasp on some necessary escape.

• ❖ •

5

There

I walk into a room and immediately start to imagine everything that may have taken place there. Walls hold within the palms of their hands all the joy, hope, tragedy, fighting, love, thoughts and lies that transpire between and within individuals.

I think back through the rooms I've entered and left. You leave a piece of yourself everywhere you go. It's just a matter of those you leave behind making a choice to remember or forget. The walls do not forget and do not let the ones who walk through their spaces night and day wash your touch from their senses. You can leave, but your voice is contained within the rooms you've left behind.

Memories and movement within space are not forgotten. Like the rings of a tree, you can burn within a space the heavy circle of your presence. Those you leave behind can look at your metaphysical markings and immediately be transported to the hour when the bend of your lip inspired a smile, a kiss or a scream.

I have distinct memories of weeping within certain spaces. When I return to those spaces I can place my palm flat against the walls, and instead of feeling the hard, cold plane of brick or cement, I can feel the tender cushion of skin. And for a moment, the walls shudder and then quickly relax and level to a rhythmic calm.

Think for a moment what it would feel like to hold an echo. Because that's what it feels like when you walk into a room and feel the hand of the one that held you long ago.

Glossary

The following words are generally Urdu or Arabic in origin. In order to maintain integrity in translation and transliteration, the most common acceptable meanings and spelling configurations have been adapted.

adhan: *call to prayer*
Allahu Alim: *"Only Allah knows"*
ayah: *verse in the Qur'an*
beta/beti: *affectionate term used to denote son/daughter*
biryanee: *a rice dish usually made with meat*
channa: *roasted chick peas*
dhaif: *weak or lacking foundation. As in a "dhaif hadith".*
dupatta: *a sheer, long scarf worn with a shalwar khameez*
Fajr: *pre-dawn prayer*
Fard: *obligatory*
firnee: *porridge type of dessert*
fitna: *controversy; trouble*
Hafiz: *one who has memorized the entire Qur'an*
halva: *a dense desert made of cream, butter and nuts*
humsaf'fer: *life companion*
Imam: *one who leads prayer; a leader*
Insha'allah: *"if Allah wills"*
Jahiliyah: *the days of Ignorance: refers to the destructive and immoral life followed by the Pagans before the Qur'an was revealed*
Jumah: *Friday (as in "Jumah prayer")*

khutba: *a sermon*
kufi: *a small cap*
kurta: *shirt*
Masjid: *mosque*
Na'na / Nan'na:: *maternal grandfather / maternal grandmother*
Ni'kah: *wedding ceremony*
riba: *interest accumulated from a bank account, usury*
Shaitan: *the Devil; known as "Iblis" in the Qur'an*
shalwar khameez: *loose, baggy pants with a long tunic*
shirk: *the act of ascribing partners to God (Allah)*
Sunnah: *traditions or sayings of the Holy Prophet* Muhammad*
Surah: *a chapter of the Qur'an*
taliboon: *students*
tasbee: *prayer beads*
tipoy: *end table*
Waleema: *celebration after a wedding organized by the groom/ groom's family; according to the Sunnah, it is advisable to hold it one, two, or three days after the Ni'kah.*

Acknowledgments
⌘

I dedicate this book to the people in my life who have taught me to understand that truths will awaken in their own time, without invitation, at odd hours of the day and night. For this, they are my healers.

A sky full of thanks to my parents, Mirza Shamsheer Ali Baig and Suraiya Baig, my lifelines in this world and the Hereafter, my guides on this beautiful journey, my first teachers, my first loves.

Duas for Nan'na and Na'na Jan, Dadi'ma and Da'da Hazarat, who give without even knowing; you are my sages on century soles. Days and nights full of thanks to Yahiya Emerick, my life companion, friend of my mind, caretaker of my heart, balm for my soul, for graciously bearing with the tempest. Samina, how fortunate we are to meet again as adults, as sisters, as friends. My dear Chanda Auntie, may Allah bless your soul, you are in my heart, you are my storyteller by the seashore. Many thanks to my brother-in-law, Qasim Najar, who kindly offered to edit the final manuscripts. A bushel of the season's best grapefruits for Mr. Tony Sawyer, who has taught me that integrity is indeed a Divine virtue.

Shukran to Caterina Barone, for ten years of rescues & computer imaging expertise with the cover. Shukria to Sawleha Khanzada for her comments during the revision process. Gracias para Veronica Mitchell, for getting me out to WILL and saying (above the rim of her glasses at Cornell): *Girl, just be quiet and write.* Heartfelt thanks to Br. Mosaddeq Hossain for his sincere belief and confidence in this project from the very beginning. I whisper thank you to my nephew, Isma'il, who takes me by the hand and shows me that "it's all love" in his world. And thank you to Zerka, Mercy and Bone for their distinguished paws of approval.

⌘

"...tie your camel..."
Nothing is possible without the will of Almighty Allah.
Nothing is possible unless you take a breath and think it through.
Make provisions for yourself. Then, leave it in His Hands.
Now *that* is something to ponder.